Indiscretion

J. B. Livingsmore

Basementia

First printing 2025
Basementia Publications
Silverton, OR

Paperback ISBN: 978-1-958337-10-3
E-book ISBN: 978-1-958337-28-8

Cover photograph by Engin Akyurt (@enginakyurt) courtesy of Unsplash.

Fiction: Romance / Erotica

Warning

The story told herein is deeply offensive. If you read it, **you will be offended.** You should not read this book. No one should read this book. This book is unsuitable for decent people. This book will fill your mind with bad ideas. This book should be burned by the purifying flames, burned until it is consumed, burned in a huge pile in the town square along with all the other interesting, um, I mean, all the other *shockingly indecent* books. Cancel them! Ban them from the school library! No children should be allowed to read them, or adults either for that matter! Incendiaries for indecency! As I say this, I'm trying to peek over your shoulder to get a better look at some of the other books burning away to ashes on the latest book bonfire of your self-righteousness. Does that one say, "penis"?

Anyway. Do not read this book, I'm telling you, you'll regret it. Reading this kind of shit is a bad idea, like eating a whole tub of ice cream all by yourself: delicious at first, but then sickening later on.

All right, well, the choice is yours. You have been warned.

-The Publishers

*Dedicated to those
who have behaved badly in the past
and to those
who have loved them anyway.*

Author's Note

I wrote this book way back in the years 2001 to 2002, but then shelved the project for literally decades without ever attempting to publish it. (When you read it, I think you'll understand why.)

Like *Frankenstein* and *Lolita*, the original unpublished 2002 version of this book opened with a frame story, for the literary purpose of distancing the story's narrator from the text's writer. Decades later, as I finally prepare this manuscript for release, I have deleted the rather distracting frame story, and am instead publishing the book under a pen name. I hope the reader can understand: if you had written a book like this, you probably wouldn't publish it under your own name, either.

This book is truly terrible. I hope you will get all hot and bothered and sexy turned on when you read it. Cheers!

– J. B. Livingsmore
July, 2025

Sunset

The first time I met Nicole, I felt a really intense and instantaneous dislike for her.

I was already kind of irritated with her before I even met her that first evening. I felt unfairly burdened because George had scheduled her as a brand-new employee to start right at the same time that our customers all start arriving for dinner, instead of telling her to come in an hour or two early like he should have done if he'd given it any thought, so I could train her while business was still slow and she could familiarize herself with the job before the big rush started. George is the owner; so he's is in charge of hiring, and he sets the schedule, too. But he's also the one who signs the paychecks. I just get told, "You're training a new one tonight," and I have to deal with it.

So there I was at the beginning of the dinner rush, hoping our new employee would arrive even just a few minutes early so I'd have time to go over stuff with her before all hell broke loose.

But Nicole apparently had better things to do than make a good impression by arriving early on her first day. No, Nicky walked in fully twenty minutes after her shift had already started.

This brand-new hire just waltzed in as if she owned the place. She stood by the door, smacking a piece of gum and tapping her foot as she looked around, so that Dawn thought she was a customer and offered to seat her.

"I'm Nicky," said Nicky. "I'm supposed to, like, start working here?"

"You are?" asked Dawn, wondering if Nicky was joking.

"Yeah," said Nicky, and appeared to genuinely believe it, so Dawn brought her over to me.

I, in the meantime, was actively taking myself far too seriously, being all managerial and busy. I did that a lot in those days, I think. It's easy to take yourself far too seriously, when you work the night-shift manager position at a popular hole-in-the-wall vegetarian restaurant in the city's up-and-coming trendy district. You sometimes begin to make the mistake of thinking that you're actually somebody important. It all seemed perfectly reasonable at the time. I was cruising towards middle-class normality. I had a decent car, a cellular phone, a bank account, a credit card, and most importantly, an attractive fiancée. She and I had even talked about making plans to take out some loans to buy a house that would be a good place to raise the children we had been discussing. I was well on my way to becoming a very serious person.

Now, the restaurant where I worked has a very relaxed dress code. Our staff regularly came to work in the full regalia of hippies and punk rockers, complete with piercings, tattoos, dyed hair, tight clothes, all kinds of stuff, none of this was a problem. For the most part, the boss didn't seem to give a damn what people wore. One time, a male waiter showed up to work in a skirt, wearing eyeshadow, and I don't think old George so much as looked at the guy twice.

The owner was however quite particular about just a few things. Midriffs were to be covered; shoes must be flat-soled and have closed toes, to cover employees' feet and protect them from falling objects and boiling liquids; and shorts or skirts should cover at least three quarters of a person's thigh.

I know I sound pedantic about this, but honestly, it was my job. George actually had some little flyers printed with our dress code, and he always makes a point of going over it thoroughly with every new hire at their interview. This is why I was more than a little surprised to see that Nicky's tight-fitting top was cropped high enough and her short, tight skirt rode low enough that her entire belly was bare; that she was wearing these lace-up, open-toed, high-heeled shoes; and that the aforementioned tight skirt was in fact the shortest I had seen outside of a costume party or maybe a racy movie for probably ten years. Not many women dress like that where I'm from, or at least not in the part of town where I hang out.

So here I am, the night manager, and here's my new employee, late to work, chewing gum, violating all three aspects of our dress code, and acting like she doesn't give a flying fuck about any of it.

"Are you in charge?" she said, her tone of voice implying that I was an unlikely candidate for a position of any responsibility.

"I make a valiant effort," I said. "You're late."

"Yeah," she said. I waited for her to mumble "sorry," but she said nothing.

"Next time you come in," I told her, "you should get here early enough that you can actually be on the floor and ready to work when your shift is scheduled to start."

"Yeah, OK," was all she said. She was looking across the room, to a table where several boys were seated together, talking and laughing. She stood like that for a few seconds, completely ignoring me while I tried to decide if I should send her home to change her clothes before or after I went over the basic introduction to the restaurant, its policies and layout.

She turned away from the boys abruptly and said, "So, are you done with me, or what?"

"Do you always talk to people like that?" I said.

"Like what?"

"Look, you're here to be polite to people. That's what we pay you for. You can start by being polite to me."

"Uh-huh," she said, and pulled out her cell phone, which had suddenly started ringing.

"Oh, hey," she said to her cell phone. "How are you? What? Oh, I'm at work. At the restaurant. The Wooden Spoon? Yeah, I just started tonight."

"You haven't started yet," I said, hoping it was loud enough for the person on the other end of the line to hear.

"You're doing what?" she continued, turning away and putting a hand over her free ear. "Not right now, I have to, you know, stay and work for a while. Maybe later. Nine? Sure, sounds good."

"You're scheduled until ten," I said.

"Uh-huh," she said to the phone. "Yeah, look, I gotta go, but I'll call you later, all right? Okay, bye." She turned to me and said, "Are you always this uptight, or do you ever relax?"

How mad would George be if I fired her on the spot? Technically, I don't have the power either to hire new employees or to terminate anyone's employment; but if I fired her right now and went straight back to the office and wrote down exactly what she'd said and done, I felt confident that George, who as the owner was usually a reasonable man, could be persuaded to support my decision, which now seemed to be the only logical choice.

"Let's assume that I am always this uptight," I said. "Are you sure you want to work here?"

And then suddenly she completely threw me off guard by giving me a big grin and a wink. "Awww, I'm just kidding ya," she said in a jocular voice. "Sorry I'm late."

"Yeah, well," I grumbled, "don't do it again."

"Right," she said, and looked around. There was a long line of people waiting to be seated, and most of the tables were already full. "Do you want me to start now, or what?"

I wanted to tell her to go home and never come back, I really did. I probably would have, except then we would have been terribly short-staffed that night.

The Wooden Spoon is a small restaurant, and all the greeting, waiting, cooking and prep, drinks, cashiering, table cleaning, and dishwashing is done by a staff of five, even at our busiest times. Because the food is so good and the atmosphere is so hip, our doggedly loyal customers are willing to stand in a line that stretches out in front of the building next door and wait half an hour or more to be seated.

Unfortunately, on this particular evening, Jasmine had called in sick. I can do the work of two people, because I am good; but for some reason only four of us, plus the trainee, had been on the schedule in the first place. Maybe George was trying to skimp on staff, but this was a bad night for it, if you ask me: we should have had *extra* staff, to make up for the fact that one of us was going to have to take time out to get Nicole acquainted with her responsibilities; but it was Monday night, and Mondays were rarely so busy; and as I've already said, I didn't make the schedule. As it was, if I sent Nicole home for the evening, the rest of the shift would be a nightmare, customers would get sullen, and Matt, Carlos and I wouldn't be able to even begin our closing procedures until after we'd actually closed, so we would all end up staying really late afterwards.

So I told Nicky that she wouldn't be on the clock until she had remedied her dress code violations. Somehow she found, borrowed, or produced by magic a change of clothes, and I let her stay. I sure as hell didn't let her leave early to go meet her friend at nine, though.

*   *   *

Nicky was a part-time student at the community college, and her job at The Wooden Spoon was her second of two part-time jobs. Some of her shifts were with Josh, the other night supervisor; and sometimes she worked days with George himself, who apparently didn't mind so much about her skirt after all, from what I overheard the other waitresses saying. Consequently I did not work with Nicky very often, and when I did, I tried to ignore or avoid her as much as I could, so that several months went by before I got past my initial impression of her.

She was a competent enough waitress, and attractive enough that the male customers always gave her nice big tips. In fact I was probably the only person who ever had a problem with her; but she constantly challenged my authority. Oh, yeah, Nicky always used to talk back to me when I asked her to do things, and she continued to violate the dress code on a daily basis. She also did all those other things that are annoying when you're trying to get something done: she consistently chatted too long with customers or friends while we were busy, she showed up late for her shifts, she took cigarette breaks without telling anyone that she was going out, she talked on the phone at bad times. From my perspective as a night shift manager, she was, in many respects, a pain in the ass, and for several months I never thought of her as anything else.

Why did that change?

Looking back I can see that it was gradual. Months went by in which Nicole's antagonism to me slowly lost its intensity, until after a while it no longer seemed so deliberately spiteful and became more of almost a friendly sort of harassment, the way buddies give each other shit. Maybe we just got used to each other. Maybe I got a little more lax with my disciplinarian stance towards her behavior (because I got so sick of chewing her out all the time) and maybe she simultaneously made more of an effort to arrive at work in a timely fashion (only five minutes late instead of fifteen or twenty), and to do what needed doing when it needed to be done (instead of ignoring it in the hopes that someone else would do it).

I think what really changed things was that although Nicole continued to give me a hard time, she began to smile more while she did it. I think this trend had been in progress for some time before I finally noticed it, one night while business was slow.

Carlos the cook was doing prep work for the next day, and Amy the waitress was out back taking a prolonged smoke break with Justin the dishwasher. I was pretending to do some accounting at the front counter but really I was just spacing out & wishing I could close up the restaurant early and go home. All the tables had been wiped, all the places had been set, all the dishes had been bussed, the floor had already been swept, it was really fuckin' dead.

Only two customers had come through the door in the last two hours, a pair of star-crossed lovers who talked earnestly, gazing deep into each others' eyes over endless coffee refills. They must have only recently hooked up, I thought; perhaps that night was their first date. They listened to each other carefully and looked at each other hungrily; not like many other couples the same age who came in regularly and sat across from each other for most of a meal without saying much, allowing their attentions to wander. Fuck, I've done it, too: you just can't keep things intense all the time, it's not practical; which is why, as I mentioned, when I saw how intensely into each other these two customers were, I arrived at the presumptuous conclusion that they were just beginning their relationship.

Anyway, they had already left and been gone for a quarter of an hour, and nobody else had come in since. That's how boring and slow it was. Nicky was reading a women's magazine that a customer had left on the counter, and it was so slow that there was no point in even asking her to pretend that she had something more important to do, because at the moment, articles on weight loss and basic sexual technique disguised as groundbreaking new methods actually were probably more important than anything I could tell her to do until either some customers came in or we closed.

I actually jumped, I was so startled when the door opened and a small gang of high-school students piled boisterously through it. I looked at them, and I looked at Nicky, and she looked at me, and she smiled.

She had a nice smile.

That kind of shocked me. I had always thought of Nicky as such a sarcastic person, it was hard to reconcile my notion of her with the pleasant look I was seeing on her face. Without a word she got up, greeted our young patrons, seated them, got them menus and ice water and took their orders for coffee, ice cream and French fries. I watched her the whole time, telling myself that in doing so I was acting in my official capacity as Night Manager, assessing worker productivity.

Tonight's Nicole was a stark contrast from previous versions of the same person. For example, there had been one occasion, can't have been more than a few weeks previously, when a group of people came in on a similarly slow night, and Nicole had just sort of waved at them, apparently meant to convey, "seat yourselves," which they did; but then without looking up again, she had continued reading her book, completely ignoring the customers while they sat there, restlessly waiting to order and seriously considering leaving. They might have simply walked out if I had not come up from the back just then, to find my waitress reading implacably as a table full of people grumbled impatiently. I chewed her out severely for that, but she never seemed very impressed by my speeches. She knew what I had never told her: that I did not have the authority to terminate her employment, and she took advantage of it.

But now, on this new night, when the new Nicky actually smiled at me and rose to her task unbidden, I decided I should reward her with some positive reinforcement, to balance out all the curtailments I had lashed out at her. I believe in positive reinforcement as a managerial strategy, I think it is more effective than threats; therefore, when a rare occasion to provide positive reinforcement to a problem employee arises, it must be seized intently and examined so that its shining brightness may be understood and remembered. Okay that was a little too fucking flowery but anyway. Looking back on it, I'm astonished at myself for attaching so much importance to the incident. "Okay, so she got up and helped some customers, big fucking deal, it was her job." At the time, however, it seemed like a huge transition and a major improvement.

In that new moment when everything seemed to change, while I was trying to formulate, in my mind, what I was going to say to compliment Nicky's behavior, I continued to watch her. While I was watching her, I couldn't help but notice that she looked very nice.

I had always known, as one knows that which is inescapably obvious, that Nicole was an attractive woman of about my own age. She knew she was hot, too, which was frankly more than a little irritating, from my perspective as her supervisor. All her daily dress code violations were her way of accentuating her latent attractiveness. Her clothes would have looked really, really good on a stranger you passed on the street; but for me, they were problematic, because my boss wanted the restaurant to project a certain image, and that image was not about sex appeal, because he didn't want the customers to think he enjoyed looking at the female form, because then they would have thought he was gross and disgusting, and nobody wanted to picture him wiping the drool from his chin as he sat in his private back office smearing the spooge off his palms before he went back out into the kitchen to spoon some vegetarian cream sauce onto the gluten-free pasta. No, nobody, truly nobody wanted to picture him like that, and that's just as well, because he wasn't like that! But he was always scared to death that people might *think* that he liked women. It would be much easier for him, in his particular niche market, it would be much better for him if he was gay. George wasn't actually gay, as it happened; but he allowed the patrons to believe that he *might* be gay, because that way they would like him better. So he encouraged the male servers to wear dresses and make-up; and he made a point of asking his female employees to wear nondescript clothing, so that he wouldn't ever accidentally glance at them with any hint of desire in his eye.

Regardless, on this one particular night, Nicole was wearing a very tasteful, long flowing linen sort of skirt and some kind of tight shirt. She looked good, and that surprised me, because I had always thought of Nicole as somebody who was "not my type," you know: a woman who other men found attractive, but who didn't do it for me for whatever reason. It was impossible to deny that the customers hit on her constantly, but I just didn't think of myself as being the same kind of person as the customers. Suddenly I was actually a little disturbed to realize that my eyes were returning again and again to the outline of her ass where it pulled against her skirt when she walked and especially when she bent over, and I realized with a bit of a shock that I was the same kind of person as the customers, after all. That challenge to my self-identity was probably the precise moment when my entire life began to go into decline; but I didn't know that yet. I only knew that I could never again refute brotherhood with even the sleaziest, most unenlightened hairy, sweaty fat guy swilling piss beer in the filthiest, smelliest back-street dive bar in town.

That's how unsettling this moment was for me. I was really, truly *disturbed* to discover that I was attracted to Nicole. Maybe it shouldn't have been so surprising, but I had so totally never thought of her that way that now I was suddenly fascinated by this disconcerting new idea, and my mind kept returning to it, over and over. The unexpectedness of discovering a physical attraction towards one of my coworkers, and this specific coworker in particular, was such an aberration in what I had previously considered to be the logical and orderly reality of my life that I returned over and over again to re-examine it. In short, I couldn't stop staring at her body.

As I watched her, Nicole had poured the coffees, fixed the desserts, given the order to the cook, and walked back over to where I was sitting. Now I couldn't believe that I had never before noticed what a pleasing curve her breasts made against her shirt. I looked at her and smiled, and she looked at me and smiled, and I am certain that it was the first time we had ever smiled at each other. A little electric current ran from my eyeballs through my brain, temporarily short-circuiting my good sense.

"That's a nice skirt," I complimented her.

"Thanks," she said coyly, "is it dress-code appropriate?"

"Oh, yeah," I replied, "you could wear that one every day."

She shook her head. "No, it would get really dirty if I did that," she laughed, and sat back down to her magazine.

"Nicky," I said.

"Hmm?" she hummed, halfway looking up at me.

"Thanks for helping those people without being asked," I said, feeling foolishly stilted and awkward.

"Oh, yeah, of course," she said. "It's not like I was doing anything important!"

So we joked for a little while about what a slow night it had been, and I had just turned back to my paperwork when she said, "Brandon?" in a different tone of voice than the one she had been using.

"Yeah?" I said, looking at her. I couldn't read her expression.

"Are you married?" she asked me. My heart started beating a lot faster.

"No," I answered; which was only partially true.

I mean, the fact of the matter is that Sarah and I were *practically* married. We had been living together for years already, and we were engaged to be married, although we had not set a date for the wedding.

Sarah is a wonderful woman. She's smart, she's got a nice body, she's independent and honest and financially responsible and politically in agreement with me. She is everything I could have asked for.

Oh, yes, beautiful Sarah June, with her long wavy strawberry hair, her generous smile, and those eyes that could melt you. It's probably not healthy for me to think too much about her any more, but you know how sometimes the wrong thought just pops into your head at the wrong time? Just now I was totally caught off guard by the recollection of how good Sarah looked in her sexy nightgown... or out of it. Sarah and I had some really amazing sex together. At the time, it always seemed somehow symbolic of our relationship; one inside the other, two unified in the pursuit of the moment, togetherness as pure blissful pleasure.

But daily reality can't always be like that. You know how it is when you live together with someone: you get used to each other. After a while, each successive moment isn't a sparkling surprise anymore just because the other person is there. Sometimes you just zone out and scroll your phones or watch too much TV together. Our relationship was not enlivened by the fact that I was working nights and weekends, and Sarah had a day job on weekdays, so we rarely had days off together. Sometimes several days at a stretch would go by when we hardly saw each other, much less found time for sex; and when we did see each other, a lot of times one of us, or both of us, would be really tired, & kind of hungry, & kind of cranky. These are not conditions which encourage a relationship to flourish. When we saw each other, there was frequently business to discuss, bills & appointments & messages; until finally each saw in the other the physical embodiment of two contradictory personas: sexual satisfaction at some times, and nagglingly irksome responsibilities and even petty grievances at others.

But I didn't say any of that, when Nicole asked me her personal question. I only said, "Why do you ask?"

Nicole looked me in the eye and said, "I guess I think you deserve a good woman."

She and I gazed at one another for a brief, awkward, intense moment; or at least it felt intense to me. Then she grabbed the coffee pot and walked back out to the table with the teens.

*   *   *

I don't know what the hell kind of a bluntly personal question that was for Nicky to ask me. "Are you married?" just out of the blue like that, what the hell was she trying to do to me? I looked at her again, but she was talking to our young customers. Then I suddenly thought of something I had to do in back, and promptly left.

That night after I came home and went to bed, in the middle of the night I halfway woke up, but I was still halfway dreaming. In the dark I rolled over & wrapped Sarah in my arms, & kissed the top of her head, & for one long guilty moment I thought she was Nicole.

I don't know how to say what happened after that. The process which followed was too gradual for me to pin it down to a specific incident. Basically my brain started returning over and over again to this one very unhealthy idea. I didn't even see Nicole again for several days, but in the meantime,

20

in my mind I indulged my infatuation. That's the only way I can describe it. It was like living in an alternate reality. While my body somehow managed to get through its daily routines and the things I had to do, the whole time, while I was talking to people, conducting business, engaged in social activities or domestic tranquility, somewhere in the back of my mind I was thinking about Nicole, remembering the way she smiled at me, thinking about her body and the way her ass looked when she bent over that table. I began to fantasize about seeing her body in a different setting. I started getting erections, really solid ones, at odd times; and I'm sure that on many occasions I probably seemed distracted and spacey to the people I was talking to.

I thought about Nicole, or about my idealized fantasy notion of Nicole, so often over the next few days that I was all charged up with anticipation for some kind of intense interaction the next time I saw her.

My shift began two hours before hers, the next time we were scheduled together. I could hardly think about anything else as I awaited her arrival. I re-checked the schedule (again), I watched the clock, I ignored people who were trying to talk to me, employees and customers alike. In short, I was useless & obnoxious.

When Nicole showed up, she was ten minutes late. I tried to kind of reprimand her for it, but I tried to smile and make a lot of eye contact, too. I hoped to come off as a jovially willful man, someone fun-loving who commands respect.

She totally ignored me.

That irked me, a little bit, but I didn't want to let it show. I mean, I had some intentions, here, even if I was still trying to deny them to myself; but I knew that acting put out would not elicit the response I was seeking from her.

Instead, I adopted the winning strategy of trying to avoid her for the rest of the evening.

As luck would have it, the evening turned out to be really busy. It was impossible to avoid working next to Nicole. I tried, to the best of my ability, to just act cool, or too busy to acknowledge her, on those inevitable occasions when we had to pass each other in tight spaces. This was complicated by the thoughts I had been experiencing recently. Even though I knew it was wrong, I wanted to make some kind of contact with her: even if it was just eye contact.

Then she bumped against me.

And a few minutes after that, she bumped me again.

It was probably accidental, I told myself. After all, my co-workers and I were constantly navigating past each other in a tight space. But at the same time, I had to wonder if Nicky had bumped me intentionally; but then on the other hand I had to wonder if I was intentionally putting myself in places where she would inevitably bump me, and the guilt started; but the trouble was that I liked the feeling of her touching me, even when she merely brushed my body with hers when she passed by. The silky feeling of her skin merely when our forearms accidentally brushed each other sent a tingle of excitement through my whole body.

I shook my head and went back to the walk-in freezer for more milkshake mix. A few minutes later I was up front working with her again. We were both getting together orders for different customers.

Now, the Wooden Spoon is not a large establishment, and the vast majority of its floor space is taken up by the seating area for the customers: there's not a lot of room for the staff to move around. I was behind the counter up front, where I had just finished preparing some desserts, and I was just about to duck back in to the kitchen when Nicole passed me going the other direction, carrying a tray full of glasses. I was obliged to back up against the counter to make room for her to walk past. She turned to face away from me, and walked past me sideways; but then, just as she was directly in front of me, she paused, took a small step backwards, and pressed her whole body against mine. For one brief instant, her back made contact with my chest, I could smell whatever shampoo she used on her hair, and I tingled with surprise as her shapely ass firmly bumped me, right in my crotch. A brief instant this lasted, and no longer. Before I even fully registered the contact, she had already moved off, without looking at me or acknowledging that anything had happened. And yet, I have spent a lot of time working around other people in close quarters in a kitchen, and I can tell you for certain, nobody had ever done anything like this by accident. There could be no doubt: Nicole had bumped into me intentionally, and really quite sensually. The brief contact sent me reeling.

So after that, being a complete dumbass as I am, the next time she came my way I decided to employ my "employee positive reinforcement" tactic, and compliment her on the fact that she was doing her job. The next time she passed my way, I said, "Way to keep on truckin', Nicole."

She neither slowed her pace nor glanced in my direction.

This was made much worse when I looked around and saw three other people staring at me. They had seen the interaction, or my failed attempt to have an interaction, and were wondering why I had unnecessarily complimented somebody who we all knew was a total slacker. I felt like a pervert caught with his weenie in his hand; it started to shrink. Ashamed, I began to fear that they saw me as a sexual harasser, an unethical boss trying too hard to attract the attention of a female subordinate. Maybe that's not what they were thinking at all, but anyway, I felt like a royal idiot.

Feeling rejected and confused, I told myself I was thinking too much about unimportant little details like this. "Stop being overly reactive," I thought, "or you'll end up acting like a real dumbass."

Following quickly on this train of thought came the first wave of an ocean of self-implication, self-loathing, and guilt, guilt, guilt. Seeing myself through the eyes of my other coworkers, I suddenly realized the sick, dirty, creepy truth about what sort of intentions I had been secretly nurturing over the course of the last several days towards sexy little Nicky the waitress. In the shock of that moment, as I recognized the disgusting true nature of my inappropriate and base desires, I imagined the scathing views of a judge or priest or righteous mother offering commentary on my lascivious drives, delivering censorious dictates against my secret desire for a clandestine liaison with this woman who was someone other than my betrothed.

I had felt desire for something forbidden. Was there something wrong with me? The fear gnawed at my soul like a sharp-toothed demon. Lying awake in bed that night, I continued to focus and fret on this issue. My guilty conscience impaled my soul on a hell-fire-hot skewer of molten moral metal, sentencing me to an eternity of torments worse than those reserved for the coldest of the cold-blooded killers; for there I was, in bed with my fiancée, sharing body heat with a woman who loved me, to whom I had pledged vows of permanent fidelity. I was in a relationship with a woman who had no major flaws, a woman who had promised herself to me and made sweet love to me. This situation was precious and hard-won: and instead of cherishing it as I should have, here I was, harboring smutty intentions that would ruin the whole thing.

I recognized this, and I knew it was wrong; but knowing that it was wrong didn't make my smutty intentions go away.

So I beat myself up, in my mind, for even *contemplating* such a brutally dishonest course of action as some of the thoughts that I had recently entertained. I psychologically slapped myself for my failed attempt to speak to Nicole that night at work; I rammed my own gut for pursuing my dirty thoughts; I kicked myself for doing it in a way that allowed me to be rejected in a public setting. I had been put off; therefore, it seemed I had committing a double wrong: first by turning my back on something good; and then by trying to force my naked desires upon an unwilling and uninterested... co-worker.

I felt sick with self-loathing. I didn't cut myself any slack for the fact that my private obsession had never really left the realm of the cerebral; I gave myself no credit for the words I had addressed to Nicky, even though they had been properly mundane, and my actions had never crossed the line into the inappropriate.

I want a cheese sandwich.

The only sexual contact I'd had with anyone other than Sarah for more than two years had been inside my mind. Despite this relative innocence, I chastised myself as if I had already committed the sin of adultery – and thus I assumed, in some ways, that it would eventually come to pass.

Logically, the slight embarrassment of this total non-incident should have killed any lingering vestiges of the inappropriate romantic infatuation from which I had suffered. Unfortunately, logic has little effect on romantic infatuations. In fact, in retrospect, as I think back on it all, I see that by dwelling on my guilty feelings, I nurtured the emotion. By focusing my mind for so long on the fear that I might sin, I eventually made the sin inevitable.

*   *   *

Well, I don't know if it was cause or effect, or maybe both; but at about that time, my relationship with Sarah deteriorated noticeably. The trend had begun some weeks earlier, but it became more obvious in the days right around the time of that same "keep on truckin'" non-incident with Nicole.

You know how it is with relationships. Whether it's going well or not, a relationship is not something concrete you can put your finger on, it's more of a vibe, an energy that flows between two people, and the energy between Sarah and me was always very potent, so strong that it was almost tangible. When everything is going well & we're getting along great, nothing can be better than the powerful flow of energy between us. It's vibrant, it slams your brain into a tingling sort of wide-awake and blissed-out feeling.

But when a certain amount of dirt gets mixed in with that nice clean energy, it can start to grate like grit in your K-Y; what was so pleasant suddenly has some bad feelings mixed in with it; and that *zing* you used to get just from making eye contact slowly turns into a heavy sludge, a guilty weight of mud poured over your head, piled over your body & oppressing your breathing until you just want to get away.

Maybe that dirt was introduced into my hitherto smooth relationship with Sarah by my feelings of guilt relating to my attraction to another woman. Maybe I allowed myself to feel attracted to Nicole because something had already gone wrong in my relationship with Sarah. I don't know. Maybe it started because I was distracted, on some occasion when Sarah wanted me to be more attentive, if she was talking to me and I wasn't in a listening mood, much less an engage-and-respond sort of mood; I don't know, man, it could have been anything. I'm telling you about a gradual shift in climate; you don't recognize the beginning or the end, and you can never say what stage of the gradient you're at, but when you've gone a long way through it, you can look back and see that the overall change has been extreme.

So things in my long-term relationship with Sarah had probably been deteriorating for a while already by the time I finally noticed. When did I become aware of it? I probably first consciously thought to myself that my relationship with Sarah had changed on one occasion when she started an argument with me, I think it was about a phone bill that was five days late because I hadn't bought stamps when I said I was going to, or some shit like that, and then she started talking about the detrimental effect that my financial irresponsibility was going to have on our children, and I was like, "Whoah there! Just a late phone bill, here, not the end of the world." My response didn't help the situation, she didn't appreciate my attitude, and then we ended up having another one of those fucking three hour conversations that never get resolved. You know the kind? Well, eventually, she stormed out of the house, and she hadn't come back by the time I left for work that night. The whole encounter left us both feeling like we didn't want to talk to each other again for a little while.

So Sarah and I didn't talk, for a while. It happened pretty easily with the schedule we were keeping. We'd exchange brief pleasantries like, "Hi," "Thanks for shopping," and "See you tonight/tomorrow." Beyond that, the simmering grievance between us continued for much longer than we should have let it go on. Rather than resolve it and put it behind us, we allowed it to fester; we each privately nurtured it by rehearsing our own internal narrative about why the other person was at fault: and in the meantime, we had very little contact with each other.

*   *   *

Less contact with Sarah left me with a lot more time to think about Nicole. One morning, as I lay in bed alone after Sarah had left for work, I masturbated to a fantasy about Nicole. It was so exciting that later that afternoon, before work, I repeated the performance.

The day after that, I saw Nicole in person.

By this time I was high-strung and sleep-deprived. My five o'clock shadow was edging on towards a week old, and my jaw muscles hurt from the way I kept clenching them all the time. I probably didn't smile very often, and I was pretty sarcastic in what I said to people.

I had resolved to myself to be straight-up brusque to Nicky. Making eyes at her as I had was inappropriate, had caused me nothing but trouble and could never result in any positive outcome anyway. Besides, since she had been rude to me the last time I'd seen her, I figured that being rude back to her was what she deserved from me.

My resolve lasted less than five minutes after her shift had started.

She was early for her shift, which was shocking in and of itself. I avoided her as she came in, I was talking to a customer or something. She went in the back to get ready, and when she came out on the floor she said, "Hi" to me, and smiled. I kind of nodded at her, and said, "Howdy," and went in back, to my office.

I sat down at my desk (well, George's desk, but I use it during my shift) and stared at the wall for two minutes. I had just started to shuffle through some papers when I head a "knock-knock" on the door. I looked over my shoulder, and there was Nicole's head, poking through my doorway.

"Hi, Nicole," I said, and looked back down at my papers.

"Brandon?" she said.

"Yeah, what's up?" I asked. I set down a page as if I had just made some sort of strong bit of definitive managerial decision-making. Then I turned my revolving chair to face her.

"I just wanted to say 'sorry' for being rude the other day, last week, whenever it was. I was, well, I was having a bad day, but I, well it wasn't *your* problem."

Fuck.

So there I was, sitting in my office, talking to my irresponsible yet somehow fatally attractive co-worker, my dick still tingling from thinking about her the day before. I wanted to say a lot of things to her, but none of them were the right thing to say. I think I just stupidly stared at her for a few, and finally mumbled something like, "Uh, thanks." I looked her in the eye, and she looked at me, and we looked at each other for a few seconds too long. I was remembering how sensually she had bumped into my body, on that same night she was talking about; and I thought that she was probably remembering it, too. Those two dissonant aspects of that evening had disagreed with each other, should have been mutually exclusive, yet somehow they had coexisted, each circumstance making the other that much more perturbing. The flirting, the cold shoulder, within minutes of each other, and repeat. Why? I will never understand *people!*

Now here she was, apologizing for the cold shoulder. I willed myself to avoid responding in a way that would reveal weakness; so instead I hardly responded at all. We continued to look at each other, a simple act which grew more exciting as it became more uncomfortable. Suddenly I knew that she knew all my secret desires, and she didn't mind.

I looked away. "Anyway, thanks for apologizing," I said, and cleared my throat, and acted like I was trying to find a certain piece of paper out of a disorganized pile of invoices and correspondence, but I couldn't find it because I wasn't really looking for anything in particular.

In a soft voice she said, "Thanks for being such a nice manager."

I looked back over at her. She had stepped into the middle of the room, was in fact standing quite close to me. She wore her blonde hair down, and some dangly jewelry. She was again wearing her long, flowy skirt that I liked, and I could clearly see that she wore no bra underneath her tight pastel spaghetti-strap shirt.

I think it was the shirt that doomed me. Having noticed it, I found it very difficult to keep myself from noticing it again and again: which is to say in all honesty that without meaning to I started staring at her breasts, they were so perky and round, and as she wasn't wearing a bra, I could clearly see the nubbins of her nipples where they pressed against the fabric.

I found myself smiling at her, despite my intentions to the contrary. "Sometimes," I told her jokingly, "I think I'm way too nice of a manager."

"No," she pouted, "most of the time you're just plain mean." She stuck out her lower lip in a sultry pose.

"Not mean enough, apparently," I said. "I don't get enough respect from employees like you; and that can only mean that I'm far, far too nice."

"Oh yeah?" she challenged me in an excitingly silky undertone. "And what is it that you do for your employees that is so nice?" Or maybe it was, "Why don't you show me just how nice you can be?" except I don't think that was it. I don't remember exactly what she said; but whatever the actual words were, somehow with her voice and her eyes and her breasts and her hips, she managed to make it pretty suggestive: and there I was, totally surprised, with my boner tugging at my boxers just wrong, so that I squirmed uncomfortably in my chair. I wanted to just grab it and adjust; but that would surely have been extraordinarily inappropriate in front of a female employee. I looked away, and couldn't think of anything brilliant or witty to say.

"I hear you're engaged," she said conversationally, abruptly changing the subject.

"Yes," I said defensively, "yes I am." I was remembering that I hadn't told her about Sarah earlier, when she'd asked if I was married; but of course people on staff are always more than happy to gossip about each other. "Her name is Sarah, and we've been together for more than three years now."

"Well, congratulations," she said, and continued to gaze at me for a while. Then she stepped back a little bit and asked, "Are you going to be a good husband?"

I was just about to say, "What the hell kind of a question is that?" when the phone on my desk rang. That phone is a business only line. All public calls ring at the phone up front by the cash register; the phone in back is an unlisted number. I looked back and forth between Nicky and the phone, then picked up the receiver, saying, "I'll talk to you later" to her before I said, "Wooden Spoon, this is Brandon," into the mouthpiece. Sometimes, somehow, (and I will never understand how) too often the public manages to get through to this unlisted line, so I was half expecting to be taking a dinner reservation or telling some slow-speaking dumbass that we close at midnight.

It was Sarah. My own fiancée was calling on the business line.

And meanwhile, Nicole was still just standing there in front of me.

"Hey, Sarah, how's it going?" I said.

Nicole made no sign of leaving. I looked her in the eye. She just stood there and looked back at me.

"Yeah, I think I put it in the cabinet next to the refrigerator," I said to Sarah. Nicole was smiling mischievously. My heart was pounding.

I don't think I'm going to try to reconstruct conversations all the time because obviously I am more or less making some of these details up. I can't pretend that I perfectly remember what exactly was said by who and to whom at precisely what time. I mean, I might remember the gist of what we discussed: but all the exact words to actual conversations, years later, I don't know, that's what you might call tricky. The steel trap that is my mind is probably just a little too rusty for precision & reliability in the total recall department. It's been a while since all this happened, and I'm all messed up right now. My brain has been been burned and fried and drowned too hard and too long throughout all of this self-pitying downward spiral, and my memory is sometimes hazy. I can never forget the solid facts; but as far as the little details are concerned, the distinction between reality and realistic imagination has become blurred.

I'll try to stick to reality.

Here's what was real, I'm not making this up. I remember what was on the wall behind Nicole while I was talking on the phone to Sarah. It had been there for as long as I'd worked at the Wooden Spoon, and I'd hated it the whole time. It was a germ-buster poster advertisement for a disinfectant soap; it said something about having a kitchen so clean that it "Sparkles and Shines!" It seemed too business-related for a room that was off limits to public scrutiny. Our decorations in this space should have been more *fun*, I felt. But now as I looked back and forth between the soap advertisement and Nicky loitering next to it, and I got caught up in a train of thought about how nice she looked next to that slogan, because she was so fresh-faced and pretty, with her sparkly jewelry and her smug smile. It was too perfect: the poster became Nicky propaganda, proclaiming for all to see that she "Sparkles and Shines!" I was inattentive to my conversation with Sarah because I was so focused on looking at Nicole; and the conversation didn't last long, but Nicky waited in my office during the whole thing, all the way through the "Love you, bye," at the end.

I hung up the phone and said, "That was Sarah."

"I gathered," said Nicole.

"Don't you have some tables to wait?" I asked her with a smile.

She grinned, then said, "Will you let me buy you a drink sometime?"

I nodded slowly. So that's how it was going to be. "All right," I agreed.

"When do you think you'll have time?" she pressed.

I thought about it. "You're closing tonight, aren't you?" She nodded. "If we're real quick about it, we can get out of here with plenty of time to get a drink or two at the Blue Brew next door before they close."

"Yeah, okay, but we never close that fast," she objected.

"Well," I said, "we'll just have to get out of here early!"

So that's what we did. Let me tell you, I think that was the fastest close I've ever done. Usually, by the time the restaurant closes for the night I've only completed a few of the closing procedures, and I don't really get around to most of the rest of the stuff, especially the accounting, until after the customers have left, which is why I often don't get out of there until after one in the morning, because I am slow and easily distracted.

But on that night, I was on it. I rode the dishwashers, called them in off smoke breaks, even helped them in the dishroom, to get their job done early; and I had already counted most of the money in the till by the time we closed, which only left me with a few last-minute things like locking the money in the safe. By the time I'd gotten done with all those things, Nicky and the other waitresses had wiped down all the tables and mopped the floor and I think we were out of there by quarter past. It certainly helped that business had been slow that night: but it helped even more that I was especially motivated.

Nicky and I hastened next door to the Blue Brew, where we managed to hurriedly gulp down I think four drinks apiece before the bar closed at two. We were alternating beer with strong mixed drinks to ensure that the alcohol would affect us, which it certainly did, most effectively. The bar was noisy and smoky. There was a stereo system blasting some raucous music so loudly that all the patrons were shouting just to barely be heard over it.

Between the stereo and all those shouting drunk people, it became necessary for Nicole and me to put our faces very close to each other in order to hear each other. Slightly unsteadied by alcohol and hormones, occasionally we pressed our cheeks together for almost accidental and brief moments. A few times she brushed my ear with her lips while she was talking to me, and after she'd done it a few times I tried it once or twice, brushed her ear with my own lips, maybe not wholly accidentally. The liquid courage I had just finished drinking was giving some credence to the fuzzy logic in my head which somehow legitimized my continued pursuit of Nicky; this same logic discouraged me from engaging in analysis, in favor of some hard-boiled action.

We were sitting pretty close. We had a small table in a corner with a bench, and we'd turned towards each other and leaned together until our knees were touching, and sometimes our elbows or our shoulders, too, and I don't remember what we talked about, but we made a lot of eye contact and smiled a lot and oh my god I felt so goddamn *horny* that finally my drunken "live for the moment" rationale prevailed over my good sense, and during a lull in the conversation, I brazenly slipped my arm around Nicole's waist.

She didn't really respond, but looked at me with a suspicious expression.

I left my arm where it was.

"And what would Sarah think about that?" she asked presently.

"Sarah, she probably wouldn't like it, no," I admitted after some hesitation.

"Then why are you doing it?"

"Well, I like it."

Nicole was still for a few seconds, but then she grabbed my hand with hers, squeezed it once, and removed my arm. "I don't know if I want to get involved in a relationship with you, Brandon," she said. "I don't know what kind of a relationship we could have, since you are already engaged to be married. I mean, obviously, I like you as a person, and if it was just about you and me, then things would be different, but as it is..." she let her voice trail off and looked away. The jukebox was playing some aggro punk rock that was totally inappropriate to the moment.

Okay, I thought to myself, *that was a bit dramatic.* I had been told off. But then I wondered, why had she asked me to come out to the bar with her and more or less encouraged me to cross some lines, if she didn't want me to? She knew, before she invited me to go out with her, that I was already involved with another woman. And yet, the whole evening, Nicole had given off the distinct impression that she wanted to get more involved with me anyway. Women. You have to believe there's some logic in what they do: but it shifts, and you can't keep track of it.

"Well," I asked, perhaps just a trifle belligerently, "what do you want from me, then?"

"Nothing," she protested, looking kind of angry and pulling away from me. "I just want you to be my friend. I just want to have a conversation and a drink."

I felt as if my desires had been not only denied, but vilified as well. It's not a form of criticism I have ever endured graciously. Suddenly I started feeling belligerently that if I wasn't going to get anywhere with Nicky, then there was no point in fighting the urge to argue with her, which was how I always felt around her anyway, so I spat out the first bullshit that popped into my head:

"Okay, wait a minute. What was that whole thing in my office, then? You can't tell me that was about wanting to have a conversation. The way you were standing there and looking at me..."

"Men," Nicole said contemptuously aside to the wall or perhaps to a hidden camera that I couldn't see; then she turned her scowl on me. "Is that really all you're interested in?"

"Hey, now, we've been talking about all kinds of other-"

"You know damn well that I want it too, you bastard," she accused. The voice she said it in was caustic and angry, which almost made me inclined to argue with her some more; but her words were incongruous with her tone, and actually contradicted what she had just been saying a moment previously: and in fact, as far as my insidious sexual purposes were concerned, these were actually the words I wanted to hear.

She wanted it, too! That blunt admission was no protestation of innocence. I like that in a woman.

So I put my arm around her again, and this time I pulled her close to me. She leaned her head against my chest. I could feel her hair pressed into my chin, the rising and falling of her breathing under my arm.

All right, enough of that already. We got all snuggly for a little while, and then the bar closed and kicked us out.

"Well, good night, then," she said to me outside the door, but she was standing much too close to me, her lips almost touching my cheek as she spoke softly into my ear, her breath warm on my neck in the night air.

I ignored her words and planted my lips decisively against hers. Her mouth moved against mine, opening so she could suck on one of my lips, and she reached her arms around my back until we were holding each other tight and kissing hard until suddenly she pulled away and stepped back again.

I could only think of one thing to do: keep going. For whatever reason, instead of walking away and going back to the comfortable life I had been trying so hard to construct with someone who loved me deeply and trusted me implicitly, the one thing I could think of was to tell Nicole the truth, to win her over with passion and honesty, to convince her to go to bed with me.

"I know it's inappropriate," I began. "I mean, first of all, I'm your supervisor at work, and getting involved in any way is a bad idea, based solely on that. And then, as you pointed out, I am already involved in a relationship with someone else, and the fact that I just kissed you would be likely to make her very unhappy, which presents a variety of issues right there. I don't know what's going to happen," I continued, moving closer to Nicole, looking her unsteadily in the eyes, "and I'm not entirely sure what would be a good idea at this point; and if I did know, I'm not sure that the good idea is what I would actually want to do. All I know," I said in a softer voice now, moving even closer. As we swayed there on the sidewalk, her nipples brushed my chest. She didn't back away. Instead, she looked up into my face with those wide eyes of hers. "All I know," I repeated, in a low voice, my mouth very close to her ear, "is that you are one of the most beautiful women I have ever met in my entire life, and in the last week or two, no matter how frustrated you make me feel sometimes, I have not been able to stop thinking about you. At work, at home, driving my car, I've been thinking of you all the time. I don't know why."

Nicole brazenly placed her hand on my belly and asked, "What do you think about, when you think about me?"

I was too caught up in the moment to moderate my reply.

I took the hand that she had placed on my belly, and I moved it around to the small of my back, just above my ass. She left it there, and then slowly, almost reluctantly, she put her other hand right on my ass itself. In response, I wrapped both my arms around her and pulled her in close, until our bodies were pressed tightly against each other. I could feel her breath, warm against my neck.

"I think about how much I want to make love to you," I confessed in a deep voice, murmuring in her ear, my cheek pressed against her face. "I think of how beautiful you must be when you don't have any clothes on, and I think of how much I would enjoy touching you. The other day I spent a long time masturbating and thinking about you and imagining what it would be like with you. I'm not really sure what's right or wrong, but I know that I've never met anybody like you, and I know that I want you, and I know that standing with you right now, you make me feel-"

She interrupted me, not with the slap I had expected, but by pressing her mouth against mine again. This made it difficult for me to continue speaking, but I didn't mind, because speaking was not my primary interest.

We stood there on the sidewalk, kissing and stroking each other for a long time. There was not a lot of traffic in that part of town at that time of night, and the traffic that did go past, we just ignored the headlights, we didn't even care.

After this had gone on for some time and we were both feeling pretty turned on, Nicole suddenly pulled away from me.

"What is it?" I asked.

In each of her hands, she held one of mine. "We can't stay here," she said. "Where are we going to go?"

It required very little discussion. Obviously we couldn't go back to my place, because Sarah was there; and the back seat of a car would not allow us sufficient space to really enjoy each other. We would have to go back to Nicole's apartment.

She drove in her car, and I followed in my own. Behind the wheel I didn't feel so intoxicated any more. I told myself that I was steady and sober enough to drive, although in truth my reflexes had probably been slowed enough that I did not belong behind the wheel of a motor vehicle.

In the car my mind had some time and space to reflect on what I was doing. *This is stupid*, I thought.

But it's okay, said another part of my brain, *because what I do with Nicole does not mean that I love Sarah any less.*

Then, *but if you really wanted to show Sarah that you love her, then you will be as faithful to her as she wants you to be*, said the more reasonable part of my brain as I sat behind the steering wheel, following Nicole to her house with the express intention of cheating on Sarah.

But, protested the impulsive and emotional part of my brain, which was really looking forward to holding Nicole's bare tits in my hands, among other things, and which was therefore willing to make up all kinds of excuses and lies to justify doing whatever the hell I wanted to do, *but Sarah knows that I love her more than I could ever love anyone else.*

Oh, argued the decent side, *but she will have doubts after this, and for good reason.*

What if I just don't tell her?

But you have to tell her.

Yeah, you're right, I admitted, I will have to tell her.

And when you tell her, she's going to be very upset.

Yes, she'll be upset.

She might leave you. In fact, it's almost certain. She will probably leave you.

No, I told myself, I'll make Sarah understand that I love her more than I could ever love anybody else, and that what I do with other people doesn't change how I feel about her.

Nicole's apartment was dark when we got there. She lived in an apartment complex with a complicated series of super-security entrance procedures which I totally failed to comprehend on my first visit. "We have to be quiet," she whispered to me as she unlocked the door to her unit, "because I don't want to wake up Becky." I decided it was reasonable to assume that Becky was Nicole's roommate. We went through the door. Inside the apartment, Nicky squeezed my hand, then disappeared inside a dark room. I was left standing next to a table which might have been the dining-room table if it hadn't been piled high with books, papers, magazines and catalogs. I looked at one of the books and saw with horror that it was titled, *The Complete Astrology Reference Guide*. As Nicky came out of the dark room, I said, "You don't really believe in this stuff, do you?"

"It's Becky's," she said, without indicating her own personal views. "Here you go." She handed me a drink. "Come on." She tugged my hand and led me through her apartment to her bedroom. I had to ask her to pause to show me the way to the bathroom first.

The bathroom was full of girlie stuff, scented soaps, exfoliants and loofahs, perfume, tampons, cremes in jars and plastic tubes, and a slightly soggy women's magazine on the floor. It featured an article which claimed to offer the secrets to the best sex of your life, which I was briefly tempted to peruse; but I had read such articles before, and they rarely discussed anything even extraordinarily imaginative, and almost never anything I had not already tried. Now was not the time for such literature.

I turned off the bathroom light and stepped out into the hallway, which was now very dark. Unseeing, I kicked something heavy, which hurt my toe and made a lot of noise as it fell over. Attempting to get around it, I discovered that it was a bicycle, and I nearly fell over it again before I managed to right it and make it lean against the wall in such a way that the hallway was sufficiently unobstructed that I could pass by without sustaining any further injuries.

My eyes were beginning to adjust to the darkness. I could sense that I was passing a doorway, with magazine pages stuck to the door, behind which I detected a faint stirring. The light in this room was off and the door was closed tightly; presumably the stirring sound was caused by Nicole's as yet faceless roommate, whose sleep I had disturbed with the nocturnal noise of crashing bicycles in the darkened hallway. Embarrassed, I hastened carefully to a faint light at the end of the hallway. The light came from around the corner. Following it, I found an open door.

I entered the room as though walking through a portal into a new dimension of my life. The light was a warm soft glow from several candles which Nicky had lit and placed around the room. Her bedroom was in an intermediary stage between tidiness and disorderliness, and it featured a large number of photographs. In places, snapshots covered the walls almost like splotchy wallpaper.

It was, however, not the room which captured my attention at that time, but Nicole herself. She had changed out of her work clothes and was now wearing a nightgown, white and loose-fitting, which managed to emphasize her comely figure while simultaneously lending her a renewed sense of erotic mystery.

We stared at each other from across the room for a minute before Nicky broke the silence by saying, "Now it's my turn. I'll be back in a minute."

I was left alone in Nicole's room with her photographs and candles and soft, unmade bed. I sat on the bed and looked at the photos, which were apparently of Nicole's family and friends. Nicole appeared in some, often surrounded by a group of young men. I could see that she had worn several different hair styles and colors in the past few years. In most of the pictures, she must have been the photographer. Some were scenes from nature hikes, others appeared to have been taken at parties, concerts and family get-togethers. I did not recognize any of the faces, and would soon have lost interest if my attention had not been caught by the image of another young woman who, I noticed, appeared in several photos with Nicole: some of which looked like they had been taken here, in this very apartment. This other young woman was easily just as beautiful as Nicole, but in a subtler, more natural way. Her hair was black and curly, her skin was dark and apparently freckled, her eyes were large and round. I wondered if these photos were of the roommate who Nicole had mentioned. I have always been bad with names but I thought I remembered Nicky saying that her roommate's name was Becky. I found myself wishing that *she* worked at the Wooden Spoon.

That was when I started to wonder if maybe I really am just an intrinsically bad person. I mean, there I was in a co-worker's bedroom, preparing to cheat on my fiancée, and even in that moment, crossing my mind like a 'possum on a busy road were lustful thoughts about a third woman who I'd never even met.

I decided to try to stick to just one infidelity at a time. Nicky would be back soon. What should I be doing when she walked into the room? Should I be sitting on the bed, fully clothed, as she had left me? Should I be standing in the center of the room, fully naked? No. I wasn't sure.

I slowly took off my jacket, then my shoes, and then my socks.

I downed the drink Nicole had poured for me, a rum and coke, it was quite strong.

I hesitated, then; and as I was hesitating I heard faint footsteps in the hallway. I tucked my socks inside my shoes, and hid my shoes under my jacket in a corner of the room. I stood in front of the doorway, anticipating its opening, preparing myself for Nicole's return.

Imagine my surprise when the face which peeked around the door was not Nicole's! I nearly grabbed her anyway, before my brain made the connection and I stopped myself in time. The girl in the doorway looked sleepy, recently awakened, her curly black hair in disheveled disarray about her dark-complexioned, faintly freckled face. The face peering around the door was the face I had just been noticing in the photographs: this must be Becky the roommate who stood before me, somewhat surprised that I was not Nicole.

Becky was shorter than I had realized from the pictures, and even in her sleepy state she was notably sexier than the photos on the wall revealed, for she had been making faces in most of the ones featuring her. In person, it was instantly apparent that she possessed a body that any man would want to, er, possess in a different way.

All manner of inappropriate thoughts crossed my mind. I was sufficiently inebriated, and far enough away from the life that to me is "normal," that I almost said something to her that would have been the wrong thing to say under any circumstances. Fortunately, she spoke first.

"Sorry," she said, "I thought Nicky would be in here." Her voice was a soft slightly scratchy alto, such a sexy bedroom voice as might be featured in the dub-over for a bad movie...

"She's using the restroom," I managed to respond.

"Oh," she said, looking at me and presumably wondering what the fuck I was doing in her roommate's bedroom in the middle of the night. The conclusion was probably pretty obvious, and from the expression on her face, she must have reached it quickly. Then she took the friendly tactic, and introduced herself to me.

"Hi," she said, "I'm Becky. I'm Nicole's roommate."

"Hi, Becky," I said, and not knowing what else to do, I shook her hand. "I'm Brandon. I'm, uh, I'm Nicole's, uh, I work with Nicole at the restaurant."

"Nice to meet you, Brandon," she said.

She held on to my hand longer than is customary for a typical handshake. I didn't want to be the first to let go. We looked at each other for a long moment. A jolt of attraction went through me like an electrical current, making my hair stand on end, sending a shocking charge down my spine and through my appendages. Becky's face was round and freckled, her eyes large and dark, her lips broad and lusciously tantalizing. Just from her appearance it was obvious that she was precisely the kind of girl I would normally consider "my type," and I knew with instantaneous and absolute certainty that I too was someone she would consider "her type" in a romantic sense. In my mind I went through a series of rapid calculations, contrasting Becky to Nicole. Though I found Nicole very attractive, her attitudes, mannerisms, and clothing style belonged to a slightly different subset of American culture; and though she was incredibly beautiful, for whatever reason I don't usually date blondes. Nicole and I didn't belong together, but we were attracted to each other for that very reason: the wrongness itself was kinda hot. Becky and I, on the other hand, looked at each other and saw instantaneously that if circumstances were a little different we would be absolutely perfect for each other in every way.

Becky had better sense than I did, though. You don't hit on the boy that your roommate has just brought home; just like you don't hit on your lover's roommate while you're out cheating on your fiancée: these are things you just don't do, because they're stupid, and they lead to trouble. Finally our hands parted. Becky coughed and looked away.

"Sorry if I woke you up," I said. "I didn't see the bike in the hallway. It was dark," I explained lamely.

"No worries," she said, "I shouldn't have left it there anyway." She paused, then seemed to feel she had to explain her presence at the moment. "I was just checking on Nicky to see how her night went."

"She's in the bathroom," I repeated unnecessarily.

"Okay," said Becky, "I'll go and see what's keeping her." She looked me in the eyes. "It was nice to meet you," she said with disarming frankness.

"Nice to meet you too," I replied in an enthusiastic mumble, trying to smile but feeling utterly confused.

I was still confused when Nicole returned to the bedroom. She had brushed her teeth and washed her face. She smelled minty and clean. She was just as beautiful as she had been before, but suddenly I was aware of minor flaws in her physique: she was maybe a little too skinny, her face pretty but very angular. I would spend the night with her; but I would be thinking of her roommate Becky.

After Nicole returned to the room, we sat on the bed and shyly talked about the decorations on the walls for a while. We started talking about a picture of her with her most recent ex-boyfriend. The conversation ended with her saying, "...but we had some really great sex together." And with those words, she gave me a big meaningful grin.

And with that, I leaned over and kissed her. She kissed me back, enthusiastically, fervently, sensually, and enfolded me in her arms and pulled me back on the bed so that I was lying on top of her, and then we were kissing passionately, exploring each other's bodies with our hands. I fondled her breasts through her nightgown and pressed my erection firmly into her abdomen. She spread her legs to allow my body between them, and I began thrusting against her with my clothes on. She broke off our kissing, then, and pushed me off her. I lay next to her, one hand sneaking inside her nightgown and resting on her inner thigh, while she unbuttoned my shirt and undid my belt buckle. I helped her to remove my clothes. When I was naked I rolled back on top of her. I already knew she wasn't wearing any underwear beneath her nightgown, which I lifted up above her hips. She put her hands on my ass and pulled me towards her as I slid inside, dangerously unprotected. She was wet, soft, smooth, tight around me as we both gasped and sighed at the intense pleasure of this contact. We quickly worked up a sweat and got her nightgown all rumpled where it was pushed up onto her belly. When I felt that I was close, I withdrew and asked, not about birth control, but if she wanted to be naked with me. We pulled her nightgown over her head. I paid some attention to her body then, sucking on her nipples and licking her clitoris, throbbing with my desire to be back inside her, while she moaned and twisted beneath my caresses. At last she shuddered in orgasm and cried out. I could wait no longer, and I put it where I wanted it. She cried out again as I entered her. Our fingers interlocked so that we were holding hands, and we kissed as we made love.

"I want to come inside you," I said in her ear. She nodded, and kissed my neck as I moved rhythmically, and she moved with me, faster and harder, and I knew I was close, and closer, until I let out a grunt of ecstasy, and she made a delightful sort of loud whimpering moan as I pushed it in as deep as I could and pumped my jizz inside her.

* * *

We lay there, naked and sweaty and breathless, not moving, each assessing the situation. Then we kissed for a long time. Though I had shriveled, I had still not withdrawn.

Then I squeezed her in a bear hug, and pressed my cheek against hers. "Nicole," I said, but didn't know what to say after that.

"Brandon," she replied, also without any additional comment.

We looked at each other for a long time without speaking. There were a lot of thoughts going through my head, things I wanted to say but wasn't sure how to make them sound appropriate. *I really hope you're clean*, was one, because we had not used a condom, and it would really suck to catch an STI. *I sure hope you're on the pill*, was another, for I was reasonably certain that she had not been wearing a diaphragm. I was also thinking such thoughts as, *What's it going to be like the next time I see you at work?* and, *I should go home now, because Sarah will be wondering what the hell I'm doing.*

Finally I said instead, "Thank you."

"What?" she said, sounding offended.

"That was real nice," I explained.

"Look," she said, "don't thank me like I'm some kind of fuckin' hooker, I won't take that kind of bullshit. It was not a business transaction." She looked genuinely angry.

"No, hold on, that's not what I meant at all."

"Well then what did you mean?" she asked suspiciously.

"I meant that I'm glad we did," I said truthfully, "and whatever happens, I'll always be glad that we did," I lied.

She looked away. "I'm glad, too," she said, but I couldn't tell if she meant it. She was not smiling. I wasn't sure what she was thinking.

Shit. It's taking me a long time to write out this whole thing. Maybe I should try to skip some of the details.

*   *   *

Well, anyway, there it is: my indiscretion. I just got done re-reading what I have so far. I think I've managed to get down the basic idea. Maybe I should have spent more time discussing my state of mind leading up to that incident, but it doesn't really matter. I just need to get the facts down.

And I have now recorded the basic facts. Here they are, you've seen it all, laid bare, spelled out, written in black ink on white paper: my first infidelity, scribbled into my notebook in shocking detail. There it is: my big secret, my lie, the beginning of all my problems.

Well, I guess I haven't gotten to the lie, yet. That was after I got back home. I crawled into bed with Sarah, hoping she wouldn't notice the smell of another woman's pussy juices on my face. She sleepily asked where I'd been, and I said I'd gone back to Joe's place for a couple of beers and a game of pool in his basement. Joe was one of the dishwashers, and it so happened that he did have a pool table in his basement, where I had gone after work at night in the past; so the story was not entirely implausible.

"I wish you had invited me," Sarah sulked. "I like to have fun sometimes, too, you know. I'm too young to spend all my evenings alone."

I looked over at the alarm clock. It was a quarter to five in the morning. I wrestled with the urge to be annoyed with Sarah for trying to monitor my activities, and for innocently believing my devious deception. I tried to make it sound as if I'd been thinking of Sarah's best interests by saying, "Honey, you have to work in the morning. I didn't think you'd want to be out this late."

Sarah said nothing for a while. I thought maybe she was falling back asleep. I put my hand between her shoulder blades and rested my head on the pillow, ready to drift off to sleep and dreams of torrid affairs.

When Sarah spoke, her voice surprised me. "Brandon," she said, interrupting my reverie, "tomorrow is my day off. We're supposed to meet my sister and her kids at the zoo in the morning. Remember?"

Well, no, of course, the truth was, meeting Jennifer and her husband Tom to look at animals in cages while their kids argued and got sticky with ice cream was one of the furthest things from my mind at the moment. This, I thought, is what you get from being involved in a serious relationship: you were obliged to waste long boring chunks of precious free time engaged in tediously tame social activities with other couples and their children. I pictured myself attending an endless string of barbecues and brunches with babies and in-laws: and I screamed inwardly.

"I'm sorry, Sarah," I mumbled into the pillow. I was remembering my hand earlier this evening as it had caressed Nicky's legs. "I totally forgot. Do we have to get there early?"

*   *   *

The day at the zoo might have started better if I'd had more sleep; or if I hadn't been out drinking and fucking the night before; or if my thoughts that morning had not been so totally fixated on my recent infidelity. As it was, I felt haggard and grouchy. I hadn't shaved, and no matter how much coffee I drank, my headache wouldn't go away.

I tried to avoid talking to Sarah's sister Jennifer. I had an irrational fear that she could read my thoughts, that when she looked into my eyes, she would immediately see that I was an unfaithful fiancé.

I didn't say much to anyone. I felt tired and irritable. I didn't want to be in company. At one point, when one of Jennifer and Tom's kids sat down on the sidewalk and refused to budge, I instantly volunteered to go back to the main entrance and rent a stroller. Jennifer was still trying to persuade little Colin that he was old enough to walk on his own two feet, and ignored me. I stood uncertainly until her husband Tom offered to come with me. I declined, "Oh, no, man, that's okay, you don't have to do that," but he insisted so that there was no polite way for me to refuse.

"Give the women some time to talk about woman things," he explained with a grin as we walked off.

"Yeah," I replied noncommittally.

Tom was ex-military, a big muscly guy with a loud voice and a confident stride. I'd met him several times but had never talked to him much. Thus his next question was probably the most personal thing he'd ever said to me.

"How you doing, there, Brandon?" he asked me.

"Kind of tired," I told him.

"Tired?"

"Had a night out last night," I admitted. "Feel like shit, actually," I said, which was true, although the hangover was only a minor factor in this.

"You look like it." Tom offered the blunt evaluation in his no-bullshit manner. He stopped walking and glanced around, then reached into an inner pocket of his jacket. "Here," he said, "world's best hangover remedy."

I stared at the object he handed to me while waiting for my sluggish neurons to identify it for me. When at last I made the connection, I gratefully unscrewed the cap from the flask. I looked around; we were by some trees behind the Reptile building, off the main path, nobody was looking. The straight alcohol nearly made me choke; it burned going down and settled in my stomach like molten lead.

"Gah!" I gasped, my eyes watering. "Thanks, I think that was exactly what I needed."

Tom tipped his head back, re-capped the flask and wiped his mouth without twitching. They teach you how to drink, in the military. "Yeah," he said, "me, too." He looked at the flask in his hand. "In fact," he said, and unscrewed the cap again. We each had another couple of pulls, while Tom made jokes about being a family man. The ice broken, we took a leisurely amble to the stroller rental booth.

I didn't see the cashier's face until we'd gotten all the way up to the desk. Tom was telling me a story about a late-night drinking session that had earned him a reprimand from a superior officer.

"Headache this big, you know, vision kind of blurry, and I've got to stand there without swaying and say, 'I'm sorry, sir, it won't happen again, sir,' and the whole time I thought I was going to..."

I stopped listening as the stroller-rental attendant looked up. I considered running away, but it was too late. She had seen me, she recognized me, she was smiling at me, oh shit.

"Hi, there," she said. "Brandon, right? I didn't expect to see you here."

"Hi, Becky," I said. Her eyes were a deep chocolate brown, her hair hung in ringlets of raven black. "I didn't, uh, expect to see you, either. Do you work here?"

"Well," she said, "usually I cashier at the gate, but today somebody didn't show up and they asked me to do strollers."

"We'd like your finest stroller, please," Tom interrupted, answering my prayer that she wouldn't say anything about Nicole.

"This is Tom," I said. "One of his kids just up and refused to budge."

Becky smiled at Tom and told him the price for a rental of the zoo's finest stroller. I fumbled with my wallet but Tom had already paid.

"All right, thank you," said Becky, handing Tom some change. "You gentlemen have a nice day. See you later?" she asked me.

I didn't know what to say. I sort of smiled, nodded, and said, "See you."

"Wow," said Tom as we walked away, he pushing the empty stroller. "Do you know that girl?"

"Not really," I said. "I just met her last night."

"You must go to the right parties," he said jovially. "She's fine! What a nice pair of-"

"Tom," I interrupted hastily, "you can't say things like that to me. You're married."

"Fuck that!" he said loudly, drawing unfriendly stares from a pair of old ladies wearing diamond-studded golden Jesus crosses on chains around their necks. "I can say whatever I like to whoever I damn well please," Tom continued. "Just because I happen to be married doesn't mean I don't notice if a woman other than my wife is physically attractive. Come on, you're practically married yourself, but you can't tell me that you didn't notice."

I reluctantly admitted that I had indeed noticed Becky.

"Of course you did!" he declared triumphantly, weaving the empty stroller between clusters of slow or stationary pedestrians. "How could you not? You'd have to be blind, or maybe gay. Seeing pretty women reminds you that you're alive! Not that I would actually *do* anything about it," he added defensively. "That's the difference with being married. You're tied down to just one woman." He grinned as we strolled past a pair of grandparents, and said, loud enough for them to hear, "Not like the old days, when chiefs and sultans and kings had lots of wives, and whole palaces full of concubines."

I smiled, the first real smile that had crossed my face that day. "Right, chief," I said.

He laughed and changed the subject, but I was still thinking about something Becky had said.

"See you later?" she had asked me, and I'd realized just how far down the road to my own personal hell I had gone, when beautiful women asking simple questions like "Are you married?" and "See you later?" could lead me to willingly destroy my own integrity so completely.

The fact was, I wanted to see Becky again, and not just as Nicole's roommate. I knew it was not at all the sort of thing I was supposed to want. Having made incredible love with Nicole just last night, it should have been her for whom my soul would branch out and blossom. And when I thought of it, I certainly felt closer to Nicole now than I ever had before, and yes, I was even looking forward to seeing her again. More than that, I should perhaps have felt something more than a shameful, regretful, conciliatory love for Sarah, who did not yet know that she had been wronged. Thanks to my religious upbringing, I was sure that I was supposed to go through some rite of penance and acts of contrition and atonement for my sins of lust, and then I would magically go back to the life I was supposed to live.

We got back to the ape exhibit, where the women had been waiting with the children. Now that we had a stroller, the kid who had earlier been screaming that he refused to take another step, was of course now running around and chasing his sibling. The women laughed about the indecisive nature of children. I shared their childish uncertainty, as I wondered if I really wanted the life that I was supposed to want; and if not, then what the fuck did I think I actually wanted instead?

The only way I could think of to see Becky again involved seeing Nicole again. Becky already knew that I'd slept with her roommate, so it seemed there was no way I could ever persuade her to go out with me. I wondered if Becky also knew that I was engaged to a woman other than Nicole; and I decided that she must, because Nicky would have told her, because women tell each other everything, don't they? *You have no chance*, I told myself. *Becky is a no go. Don't even think about trying.*

But what about Nicole, then? If the opportunity presented itself again, would I go back to her apartment again? Or would my sin be a one-off, a single solitary indiscretion?

I looked at Sarah, laughing in the sunshine beside the bonobos. She was really beautiful. I still remember the elegant fabrics she was wearing that day; I remember the fancy way she had done her hair, with small braids on either side that met in the back and somehow almost contained the cascades of her auburn tresses; I remember how the curving lines of her body were revealed by her fitted dress. I knew that despite my recent actions I truly, deeply loved Sarah and would never want to lose her. In that moment I told myself that I would reject all thoughts of Nicole in the future. In that moment I told myself that I was resolved to be a good husband to Sarah from then on and for the rest of my life.

Even so, I may have had secondary motives when I offered to take the stroller back, after another hour of gazing at Africa's endangered species and South America's biggest snakes, when the children had lost interest entirely and wanted to go home. I walked to the stroller desk with a big smile which quickly turned to a deep disappointment when I saw that Becky's seat had been taken by a pimply teenage boy. I almost glared at him, as if he were involved in a conspiracy against me.

"Thank you, sir," he said. "Have a nice day."

I nodded and walked away. *I'm supposed to be better,* I told myself. *This is the Universe, telling me that I'm supposed to be better. I have to try to be a good husband from now on.*

*   *   *

For days I had been thinking about the next time I was scheduled to see Nicole at work. I had been worrying about it, anticipating it, planning what I would say.

"We should keep our relationship professional," I rehearsed the words and practiced saying them to myself over and over on the way to work that night. I would talk to her as soon as she got there. Well, I didn't want to be rude, so first I would inquire after her well-being, so I wouldn't seem like just a callous dickhead who had just been using her for sex. I didn't want to think of myself in those terms. Then after the necessary formalities, I would clearly state my opinion that, though I liked her as a person, I felt that our liaison had been a mistake, and what we'd done could not be allowed to happen again.

But we were short-staffed at the restaurant. Matt the waiter didn't show up for his shift, and neither did Carlos the cook. Half an hour on the phone failed to locate either of them, or anybody who would be willing to cover for them. This left the prep cook doing all the line cooking, and me running back & forth between waiting tables and trying to keep up with the prep work. By the time Nicole showed up, I was deep in manager mode, and completely forgot what I'd been planning to say to her. A moderately busy night was becoming busier; we were slammed, and short-staffed, and I'd just turned on the slicer to slice some onions, and while it sliced I was mixing a drink for a customer with one hand and drinking coffee with the other hand. When the slicer got done I ran over & shut it off, then started pouring a beer from the tap. That's when Nicole walked around the corner. I hardly looked at her.

"Hey, glad you're here," I said, "we're short two tonight." As I spoke, I was putting the beer & the drink on a tray. "Will you take these out to table six please?"

That was the moment when I didn't say what I had been planning to say to her. Saying it would have been callous, and poor timing, and all kinds of bad things, and probably would have pissed her off; but *not* saying it left the possibilities open.

Open in my mind.

Nicole took the tray without saying anything. I helped in the kitchen for a few minutes, then helped in the dishroom for a few minutes, then scurried back to take out an order up. As I went through the doorway I saw Nicole at the cash register: there was a line there, waiting to pay, and another line at the door, waiting to be seated.

Jasmine was clearing tables. I took some orders, poured some coffee, and looked up to see that the line at the register was gone, as was most of the line at the door. I was impressed.

All that evening, Nicole and Jasmine and I just flew all around the place. We turned it into a kind of efficiency competition, a game, which made it seem almost fun to be working so hard. I walked around the restaurant so many times, so fast, I think I worked off all the extra calories I'd eaten with dinner. Every time we passed each other, we'd smile, trade trays, compare notes, exchange important information; we were all working together, and although it was just this side of stressful, we knew we were achieving a kind of peak performance. I smiled at Jasmine, I smiled at Nicole. Jasmine smiled back. Nicole didn't, at first, and part of my mind started to worry, while I worked, worry that she was mad at me; I contemplated all kinds of fears, rational and irrational and probable and exaggerated. I feared, for example, that Nicky would tell Jasmine that she'd slept with me, or – gods forbid – that she would tell Sarah.

I was worrying about all these things while another part of my brain was trying to ring up an order, and make change, when suddenly there was a loud crash from the kitchen, & I heard Nicole's voice exclaim loudly, "Oh, shit!" I looked up, afraid the customers would be offended by the profanity, but they thought it was funny. A table of teenage boys started clapping.

As soon as I could, I ran back in to the kitchen. Nicole was just about done cleaning up the broken glass & splattered food. She looked up as I came in. "I am so sorry," she said, "I can't believe I did that." I looked into her eyes. There was something funny about them.

"Well, you know," I said, "it happens to the best of us." I looked closer, and I was sure. She was high! Nicole had come to work high on drugs! I was torn between being irritated, as her official supervisor; or being amused, as someone who occasionally has been known to enjoy a puff just prior to a shift; and part of me was just relieved that this explained her odd behavior, and that she wasn't angry at me personally.

As I helped her finish cleaning up the mess, ensured that the cook was already working on replacement meals, and offered to talk to the table whose order we'd just finish scraping off the floor, she said, "Thank you," and gave me a really big smile. That smile meant a lot to me, more than I should have let it. But can I really blame myself? Nicole gave me the kind of smile that men dream about for weeks afterwards.

I had to smile too, as I remembered saying those very same words to Nicky when we were in bed together, and her touchy response to them at the time.

So I grinned as I answered back, "You don't have to thank me. What do you think this is, some kind of business transaction?"

Nicole laughed, and looked around to see if anyone was watching. Everyone was too busy to watch. She gave me a quick kiss on the cheek and said in my ear, "It is, but maybe I don't mind so much."

I felt a stirring in my boxer shorts. Nicole's cheek briefly touched mine. Then Jasmine came through the doors into the kitchen and we pulled apart guiltily. I don't know how Nicole felt, but I think my face was bright red as I walked out on to the floor, and I was stuttering with embarrassment when I tried to apologize to the grandparent type couple whose steaming hot dinners had just ended up in the bin with some broken plates. They were really nice about it, though, they laughed and the lady said, "I just knew it, when we heard those plates break, I said to Fred, I said, 'Fred, those were our dinners, you just wait and see.' I told him, 'That would be just our luck, wouldn't it?' Because everything has gone wrong today, the lawnmower ate the garden hose, the car broke down, and someone vandalized our mailbox, all in one day; so if anybody's dinner is going to end up on the floor, it's going to be ours. The Good Lord is testing our patience, but we've lived long enough we've learned a lot about patience, and we've both got plenty of it. Isn't that right, Fred?"

Fred looked at me and asked, "How about drinks on the house while we wait? To help us show the Good Lord how patient we are."

Fred's wife started to argue with him, but I assured them it would be no problem. I rather wanted a drink myself.

Nicole apologetically took out their drinks and, as soon as it was hot, their order. Out of the corner of my eye I saw her laughing with them about the whole thing.

The elderly couple were in a good mood. I rang them up at the end of their meal. They good-naturedly teased me about the serving help. Fred's wife leaned forward and said to me conspiratorially, "The girl who dropped our dinners really is lovely, though. Just a beautiful girl, don't you think?"

I smiled and bungled my way through something like, "Yes, we're quite happy to have Nicole with us here at the Wooden Spoon."

"Are you married?" the woman continued bluntly. Why did people keep asking me this question? I had to admit that no, I was not, yet.

"Well," she said, "you should take a good look at that waitress there, I tell you. Beautiful girl, really beautiful."

I politely agreed, remembering how beautiful Nicole had been without her clothes on, and trying to tell myself that I would stand behind my private resolution to never see her naked again.

Nicole walked up to me just as they left. "What did they say about me?" she asked.

I smiled. "They said I should marry you," I said.

Nicole laughed out loud, saying, "I don't know about that! Ha! What did you say?"

"I told them you were very good in bed," I told her in a voice that was calculated to carry no further than her ears. *Shit*, I thought after I said it, *that wasn't what I was supposed to say!*

"You did not say that," she said, sounding a little worried that I might actually be so crazy.

"What, you don't believe me?" I teased her. "I think that was just what old Fred there wanted to hear."

"You sure do know how to give a girl that warm, fuzzy feeling," she said ironically. I thought she was about to do the routine which involves the woman walking away angrily, but she hesitated, and I hurried to ask her what she thought I should have said.

"I don't know," she said, "but not *that*. You didn't really say it, did you?"

"No, of course not! My stupidity only goes so far."

"How far is that?"

"I think you know."

"And what's that supposed to mean?"

"My stupidity," I explained, "just goes far enough to make my life really complicated."

"And to complicate the lives of everyone around you."

"No," I replied thoughtfully, "only the lucky lives of a select few fortunates get pulled into the vertiginous vortex."

Nicky groaned. "How very lucky I am," she said. "Well, at least they left a decent tip," she continued a little louder, and I saw Jasmine eyeing us curiously from not far away.

"Well, that's good," I said, "maybe they'll come back. I thought they were really nice."

Jasmine seemed satisfied by this, and Nicky & I went in separate directions to take care of business.

*   *   *

Somewhere in there I made a big mistake, but it was in the form of an inaction, not an action. See, I had sworn to myself that as soon as she got there, I would make my apologies to Nicky and ask her to consider our, ah, incident to be a once-off; and then I'd broken my vow, I had said nothing, because I didn't want to say anything, because when I saw her that night, suddenly one time with her didn't seem to be enough, and I let the busy buzz of business distract me. I could have postponed my little speech until a better time, but the real reason I didn't make it was that I didn't want to.

When Nicky came in that night, when I gave her the tray with the beer and the mixed drink for table six, the sight of her had an effect on me that did not make me want to push her away in favor of another woman, regardless of prior commitments. Far from it. Seeing Nicole in person reminded me why I had desired her. I found that I wanted to indulge in luxurious sensuality with her and I wanted to make love with her again. Finally the rush of customers subsided and we began our closing procedures, and I watched the curves of

Nicky's body through her clothes as she moved; and as I watched, I remembered how wet her pussy had been...

We didn't talk about it, we simply contrived as if by chance to be the last two to leave the restaurant that night. Jasmine may have had suspicions, but I think she was so glad to go home that she didn't really think much of it.

When we were alone and everyone else had left, we went into the office. We had been discussing the final details of our closing procedures, but when we entered the door of that back room we fell silent & began kissing.

"Brandon," she said, but I held a finger to her lips, looked her in the eye and shook my head.

Neither of us said anything else until we had made love on the floor of the office, which was somewhat uncomfortable but well worth it. It was less sensual than our first encounter, less prolonged, more blatant & direct, want to fuck now, can enjoy fingertips on cheek later... We came together, voicing our climax loudly, the cries almost as of pain, unrestrained by concerns of being overheard.

Afterward I lay on top of her as we kissed. We were both panting & sweating, and I had not yet withdrawn. Neither of us had properly undressed, either.

"Brandon," she said again.

"Nicole," I said with a smile, and kissed her cheek.

"This is a bad idea," she said.

Hey, wait a minute, I thought to myself, *that was supposed to be my line!* Instead of grabbing this issue by the balls, I tried to just make a joke about it. "I'm bad, the idea is bad, but the sex is great!"

"Don't be so fucking immature, Brandon, I'm serious."

"Well, come on, now, Nicole, what am I supposed to say, I mean, I'm serious too, really, I'm just trying to be congenial about the whole thing, is that really so unreasonable?"

"Yeah, that's all you want, is to just be congenial," she accused. "You want to just have your little fling and then go back to your perfect life with everybody feeling friendly towards each other afterwards. You didn't want to make any waves. But the world doesn't work like that. What kind of person do you think I am? Do you think I'm just somebody who can be convenient for you, here when you want me, gone when you don't anymore?"

She was really angry, practically shouting at me there in the office of the deserted restaurant in the middle of the night, and I was like, whoah, girl, it's a bit early on in our relationship to be pulling this kind of dramatic shit. I should have told her so. I should have reminded her that she had just told me, "Maybe I don't mind so much." Telling Nicole that she was overreacting could have helped to make me feel like I was in control of the situation, but I felt like my reality was spinning out of control and I allowed myself to get sucked into the games we play.

So I played her game, even though it's a game she was destined to win. Should I choose to play at all, then she had already won. That was the nature of the game. I should have been in enough similar situations by my age to have this figured out; but I wasn't thinking, or I was looking for excitement, or something.

Yes, I played the game. The rule of the game is, you tell her what she wants to hear.

I'm spilling shit here. I just knocked over my fucking beer. The brown foam is oozing all over my carpet, near the congealing red splotches left from recent salsa spills.

It doesn't really matter how I sweet-talked her. In contradiction to my earlier and more rational intentions, I now did what I could to assuage Nicole's feelings. I even accepted the defensive position: I argued against her, and consequently against what I had originally thought were my own personal views.

I don't want to sit here and bloody well go through the whole thing. Anyway, the point is, like a dumbass I tried to convince Nicole that I had engaged in sexual congress with her because I liked her as a person: because she had attracted me with her uniqueness and her vivaciousness and all that shit, as well as her physical attractiveness.

And fuckin' A, here's a surprise: she wasn't satisfied by that explanation. She pointed out (truthfully) that I was not just dating but actually engaged to another woman.

I conceded that this inconvenient fact cast me in something of an unfavorable light under the present circumstances. Nevertheless, I persisted in my claims that I did in fact respect *both* of them as people.

"I love Sarah," I told Nicole. "I have always loved Sarah, and I always will. It's as if we grew up together, because in a way, we did. She is an undeniable part of my life that will never go away. But at the same time, I am still young, and she and I are not married, and lately to be perfectly honest, we haven't really made much of an effort to spend time together. As far as I'm concerned, the fact that I have acted on my attraction to you does not interfere with my love for her, just as I don't think my love for her necessarily contradicts... ah, contradicts what I want from you."

"And what is it that you want from me, Brandon?"

What kind of shit did I tell her? Did I mean it? The fucked up thing is that I probably meant all of it, every single word, meant it deep in my heart at the time when I said it. I wasn't just saying this stuff: I really thought I could just sort of without missing a beat have two girlfriends instead of just one, and I would enjoy a superabundance of great sex and somehow magically keep both of them happy.

"It kind of puts me at a disadvantage that you're already engaged, doesn't it?" she reminded me again.

"Well, what is it that you want from me, Nicole?" I countered.

Nicole didn't answer this right away. "I'm not sure I want anything from you, Brandon," she said. "I think that maybe this whole thing was a mistake."

"Everybody makes mistakes. Sometimes people continue to make the same mistake over and over for years."

"I think," she said, ignoring me, "that you think I'm just convenient for you."

And so on and so forth. If you've ever been involved in such a conversation, you know that it can last for hours; and if you haven't ever been involved in a conversation like this, then go get laid, for fuck's sake. Eventually I successfully told her what she wanted to hear; and in the process I probably ended up saying some things that were probably a really bad idea. In the end I was committed to the position of either contradicting myself or else proving what I had told her; so suddenly there I was down in it, with two girlfriends.

And that is how Nicole and I became involved in a clandestine relationship, prolonging our liaison from a one night stand into an ongoing series of meetings. It went on for months. Whenever the opportunity presented itself, we had sex together. Sometimes several days went past, once a couple weeks went by and we didn't even see each other. We were okay with this open relationship. She didn't tell me what she did at those other times; and I didn't ask. I assumed she was seeing other people, but there would have been little point in asking. She knew that I was with Sarah when I wasn't with her; and yet, Nicky and I had discovered that we enjoyed each other's company.

Nicole didn't argue with me again for a long time after that, and when I saw her it was just an easygoing and fun relaxed tempo. We didn't talk much about my relationship with Sarah. It was simply assumed, like the fact that we both had parents.

And all this time, I still didn't have the balls to tell Sarah about the whole thing.

*   *   *

That's what's bad about all this. If I had been honest with Sarah, early on, about what was going on in my life, things might have turned out differently. If I had been honest with her, then who can say? Maybe she would have been relieved. Maybe she would have said, "You know, Brandon, I've been thinking that you and I had unrealistic expectations of each other." Or, maybe she would have been okay with it. Maybe she would have *encouraged* me to have another lover, on the condition that I agreed that she could have one too. Perhaps we could have reached the understanding that she and I had a deeper more lasting commitment to each other, and what we did with our other friends could not change that. Or more likely, we would have simply ended our relationship at that time, and it would have been painful but clean, well, clea*ner*, a bit cleaner anyway, still kind of messy I guess, but even so, cleaner than how it all ended up eventually. The real point is, even if all this other stuff is crap, I know for a fact that in order to be certain that she and I both felt the same way, I would have had to be honest with Sarah, sooner into these incidents, about these incidents.

But no, even that is crap. If I'm really being honest with myself, the only thing that could have convinced Sarah of my love for her is if I'd never cheated on her in the first place.

Even so, if I'm being really, really painfully honest with myself, Sarah and I would have had some serious relationship problems, even if I had never gotten involved with Nicky! Sarah and I were already having problems before I ever kissed Nicky that first time. Our communication had been poor for a long time, we didn't see each other enough. We had fallen into a rut, and weren't making enough of an effort to get out of it. Maybe we had started out together too young, too idealistic, too friggin happy, and therefore doomed from the start.

But I didn't give Sarah the chance to surprise me with how understanding she could be. I didn't even give Sarah the chance to get hugely pissed off at me. Honestly, I was afraid that if I told Sarah about Nicole, then Sarah would leave me. Such a fear does not sound at all outside the realm of probability, does it? Leaving my cheating ass would have been her right, absolutely. Therein lies my only justification, pathetic as it may be. I lied to Sarah because I wanted to stay with her. It wasn't a good tactic, I will admit; but I can't claim to have used my brain and really thought about most of the things I did during that whole period of time. I just did things, sometimes with the full knowledge that I should not do them, always with a justification volunteering itself from the dark recesses of my mind.

No, I was dishonest, and I regret it, but I can't take it back.

And other people were dishonest with me, too, and I wish they hadn't been, but what am I going to do about it?

I'm running out of time. I've spent too much time staring at walls. I must finish writing this out, before the dawn of the new day can begin.

What you have to understand is that I wasn't actually talking to Sarah much at all during this time. I suppose I still loved her as deeply as ever; but we weren't really communicating, even when we were in proximity to each other; and increasingly, we rarely happened to be home at the same times.

And then, every so often, maybe once or twice a week or so, I would hang out with Nicky, and every time I saw her outside of work, we had a great time, I felt increasingly happy to share time with her. She was crazy and sarcastic and fun, and we had really great sex together. Had I mentioned that yet? The more we hung out together, though, the more we discovered that we really did have a lot in common, not just mutual attraction; and that our personalities, though very different, did not clash, and we actually could get along fabulously.

I soon realized that I had underestimated Nicole. Having always focused my attention on how different she seemed from me, I had never guessed that we would get along so well; but as it turned out, we got along really well and found that we really liked each other. We started doing fun things together, going for walks in the park, seeing movies sometimes, eating pizza, making love in the afternoon.

It was during one of these afternoon lovemaking sessions that Nicole first said the word "love" to me, not in the usual three word phrase but the connotation was there, and I didn't react quite the way she wanted me to. For although I genuinely liked her a lot, and I told her so, at the same time I didn't see her as my future wife or anything, and I told her that, too, and I guess she thought that was pretty rude, but I didn't mean it to be rude, I mean, I'm sure that she didn't think of me that permanently serious way either, so maybe she was just looking for an excuse to get pissed off at me. Anyway, nothing happened at that point, it just became ammunition for things that came later.

* * *

It might be my fault. I may have been the one who upset the balance. (Of course it was my fault. Everything is my fault.) At any rate I think the whole thing got messed up by my attraction to Becky.

It's inconvenient to be secretly attracted to your secret lover's housemate. The inconvenience is compounded when the housemate returns that attraction. It happened once or twice or maybe even three times that I would come over to see Nicole, and then while Nicky was in the kitchen getting a beer or something, Becky and I would start talking, and we'd just laugh and joke like old friends, and make a lot of eye contact, and agree with each other about all kinds of random things, and excite each other with our conversations on obscure subjects, sometimes to the point that Nicole probably ended up feeling totally left out when she came back into the room.

But the three of us hung out together a lot, when I was visiting Nicole, and we had a good time. It felt like such a party atmosphere that I think all three of us really started looking forward to the occasions when I would come over for a beer and stay for conversation with Nicky and Becky and conclude with some fun sex with Nicole before going home. It was a great way to spend the evening, and there was a little in it for everybody.

But then that all changed.

* * *

One night when Sarah had flown back East to see her grandparents, Nicky and Becky and I started doing tequila shots while we were in the middle of a long conversation which had included a number of extremely sexual references and stories from all three of us. We ended up polishing off the entire bottle much too fast, and we were all feeling pretty racy by then.

In the drunken warmth that followed, somehow we all ended up moving from the living room, and we were all sitting on a bed together with our shirts off, doing circular back rubs. I got all into it as I was massaging Nicole's shoulders, and I leaned forward and started kissing her, not so much her mouth because I couldn't quite reach my face around that far the way I was seated, but up and down her shoulders and neck I kissed her wetly, and sucked on her earlobes. She giggled and gasped and turned her neck so I could kiss the choicest, most delicate spots; then she pulled away from me to lean forward. Above where her fair hands were gently massaging Becky's brown and freckled shoulders, Nicole planted her lips sensually against Becky's neck. And again. And again. I scooted over on the bed so that I could keep kissing Nicole while she kissed Becky; and in doing so placed my own neck in reach of Becky's mouth, which I didn't even realize until the feeling of her mouth against my skin sent a spike of tangible euphoria tearing through my consciousness.

We all really got into it. It was an experience unlike any other I have shared with others; and even if it seems tasteless, well the whole point of this whole thing that I'm writing is that nobody else will ever read it, and in this one very special instance, I want to remember every minute detail of what happened.

We didn't discuss it; we just worked as a unit, the three of us together. As we kissed each other's bare torsos, we began to explore with our fingers and hands. I had Nicole's breasts lovingly cupped in my hands when Becky, sitting behind me, surprised me by very brazenly opening up the front of my trousers and reaching right on in.

Then we were all three helping each other out of all our clothes, laughing together until we were all naked, and kissing each other, and touching each other all over with our fingers and lips...

I don't feel like this is coming across the way it seemed at the time, because translating such an experience into words subjectifies it and taints its purity. It was possibly the most beautiful experience I will ever have. These two girls, the slender blonde one and the exquisitely curved brunette, were both seriously fucking knockout gorgeous and naked, and they were lying on their sides, fully kissing and touching each other. I lay down next to Nicole and made love to her from behind while she kissed Becky and they fondled each other. I was so turned on and Nicole was so sweetly wet that I had to fight the urge to come instantaneously, but I wanted to make it last, so I went slow, and when I was afraid I might be getting close, I pulled out, and did something else.

The three of us smiled at each other as I wiggled my way in between the two kissing women, my head at waist level, facing Nicole. I kissed her belly and thighs, running my hand over the smooth skin between her legs until my fingers found the hair of her pubic triangle. She opened her legs for me, and I kissed my way deep into her most secret places. I licked my finger for lubrication, which proved to be redundant as I slid it smoothly inside the tight warm space that my own erection had been filling mere moments before.

And all the while the two of them were kissing, touching, stroking, going at it with each other like mad.

Then I noticed that Becky was pressing her pelvis against the back of my head, and grinding on me. Still working on Nicole, I reached behind me with my other hand and found Becky's legs. I moved my hand up and down her inner thighs, appreciating their curves and smoothness. I tried to masturbate her while performing cunnilingus on Nicole, but the angle proved too awkward. Wordlessly, the girls rearranged themselves to resolve this complication. I left one finger inside Nicole and continued to move it around as I turned my face to her roommate's pussy. Becky opened her legs and I explored her with my nose and tongue, licking her labia and clitoris as I worked a finger up inside her. She wrapped her legs around my head as I built up pressure and speed in my attentions.

Then I noticed that Nicole's body wasn't moving. I still had a finger in her, but I had forgotten to maintain its circular motion. She was beginning to feel neglected. I attempted to extricate myself from the tangle of Becky's legs and move my face back over to Nicole, but as I was doing this, Nicole pushed both of us away from her, and scooted over on the bed. She spread herself out so that her body occupied most of it, her legs open wide, her arms flung out to the sides in complete abandon, the look in her eyes saying, which of you is going to prove yourself by satisfying *this*? I was just reaching for her when suddenly Becky, in the frenzy of the moment, was on top of Nicole, kissing her face, kissing her neck, kissing her breasts, her belly, her private parts; Nicole sighed and shuddered as Becky began moving her head back and forth rhythmically. While she was doing this, Becky was crouched down over Nicole with her ass in the air. Her pussy was pointed straight at me, and it was really nicely wet, I knew because my fingers and tongue had recently been right there... As I stared at her, tempted by how her pink folds were open and swollen with her desire, Becky paused in her servicing of Nicole to look at me. Nicole had her knees in the air and was quivering with excitement, but Becky broke off briefly to turn around and look at me: and then she shook it at me, yes, she smiled as she waggled her ass in the air, before she turned and buried her face back down deep into Nicole's pussy.

How much more invitation could I have needed? I began kissing the back of Becky's body, starting with the backs of her legs and proceeding through her thighs and her labia to her ass and her back, and as I kissed my way up her back, I inched my body up and over hers, until I was kissing her neck and shoulders, and my erection was right behind her. I gently brushed it against her pubic hair until it made light contact with her moist inner folds, and she moved in an unmistakable way, and I knew she wanted it, so I bit her neck and slid it in slowly, and she gasped and so did I, she was so wet and the sensation was beyond magical, it was the most intensely wonderful thing I have ever felt in my entire life.

Becky cried out, stopped working on Nicole to push back against me a few times, then cried out again as I thrust even deeper, loving her tight wetness. I kissed her cheek. Supporting herself on her elbows, she put her hand on Nicole, to free up her mouth; and I too put my hands on Nicole, to stimulate her as much as Becky's and my mutual efforts could; and at the same time, Becky and I kissed, despite the awkward angle, as I made love to her from behind, and I felt that we were really better for each other than any two humans were ever meant to be. Then Becky was rubbing her clit with her other hand, and I blew my wad inside her as she pushed back against me and cried out into my mouth, which was still locked in an embrace with hers; and we came together, kissing.

After that we worked on Nicole together, until she too shuddered and cried out.

It was a wonderful moment. I had been attracted to Becky for a long time and now I knew that she was attracted to me too and that we gelled in a way that was unbelievably good. And Nicole was just a great person to be with, funny and sexy and unpredictable. I felt love for them both and for Sarah back East with her grandparents and for the whole world. I felt that it was possible for everybody to love everybody else freely and we could all just be really really happy all the time.

Unfortunately, the two girls involved did the girl thing and worried about it for days afterwards, worried about whether it was right, worried about whether it meant the same things to each other and to me. I wasn't worried. I thought it was great. Now I had *three* girlfriends! Life couldn't be better.

*   *   *

But that situation was just too complicated to stay good indefinitely. Suddenly there were too many variables. Nicole started getting mad at me because she felt I was focusing too much attention on Becky. She brought it up to me several times but never said anything to Becky, even when I said she should; and in the meantime, if Becky was smiley and friendly with me when I came over to see Nicole, I wasn't about to be so rude as to tell her to leave me alone. Hell, Becky was super cute, and we got along really well, and we'd had some great sex together. It wasn't like I had some overwhelming commitment to Nicole or anything.

And this was eventually what Nicole claimed she wanted from me. Probably she was just unhappy in general and made this particular claim because it was easy and would sound right to fit the situation. I don't think that the fact that I got along well with Becky really bothered Nicole as much as she said it did; but she *was* disturbed that her relationship with me was, as she saw it, merely a casual sidetrack from my relationship with Sarah; and she took out her frustration on my lighthearted and fun connection to her roommate Becky, apparently because she was distraught by the ease with which the two of us bonded, even though we didn't have sex again after that one drunken tequila night. She thought my bond with Becky cheapened my bond with her. Nicole started trying to only invite me over at times when she knew that Becky would not be home. Then after a while, Nicole started inviting me over less and less at all.

*   *   *

I don't remember what day of the week it was or what circumstances surrounded the event, but there was a conversation that I had with Nicole one night that forever changed the tone of our relationship. It started off in a seemingly innocuous manner. It was mid-afternoon, and the sun shone through Nicole's bedroom window and illuminated our naked bodies, as we lay next to each other on her bed in a post-coital reverie. We started talking about the future, trading visions of where we saw ourselves in five or ten years.

"I'd like to be a model," Nicky told me. "I want to make a lot of money doing that, and maybe fashion design. I want to buy a house and a car and get married and have kids."

"Oh, yeah?" I said idly.

"Yeah," she said, "I want to get involved in a serious relationship with a man who I love, and settle down with him, and start a family."

She moved over and rested her head on my shoulder. I was starting to feel uncomfortable. Nicole's talk of starting families reminded me of similar conversations I'd had with Sarah, a thought that instantly turned this conversation into a compromising situation.

"So, what kind of guy are you going to look for?" I asked, trying to imply that, as I thought we both knew, the guy in question could never be myself.

But Nicole turned to look at me and rested the palm of her hand on my chest. "I think I'm looking for a guy kind of like you," she said. "Somebody who's sweet to me, and listens to what I say, somebody who's dependable and financially responsible; somebody who listens to cool music, who I have a lot of fun with."

"It's good to have a lot of fun with someone," I agreed, trying to think of a good way to change the subject, and completely failing to come up with anything.

"I have a lot of fun with you," said Nicole, and I groaned inwardly.

"Yeah," I said, "I have fun with you, too..." I said, wondering how I could tactfully remind her that I was already engaged to someone.

Nicole raised herself up on an elbow and looked me in the eye. "I love," she said languorously, "making love with you."

I had at first feared that she was going to say something else, and was so relieved that she had concluded her statement that way, that I readily concurred. "You and I make some really nice love together."

"It's the best," Nicky said with a grin. Though we had just completed an arduous session, Nicky climbed on top of me and did something to arouse me, looking me in the eye the whole time. I looked back, gazing into her eyes as I felt my body responding to her touches. We maintained eye contact as she straddled me and sat back against my erection; we maintained eye contact as I filled her up and she squeezed me in. She slid up and down on me, slowly, fluidly, with deliberation, as we both twitched with erotic excitement. I was unaccustomed to maintaining eye contact with anyone for so long, much less during sex. Staring into each other's eyes so intently while making love very slowly made the whole experience very intensely personal. "Nicky," I breathed, "you're so wet, you feel so good." I moved my hips around in a circle to work all her angles. She moaned and pushed back against me. Then she leaned close to my ear and whispered something I'd been afraid she might say. "I think our bodies are trying to tell us something. I make such nice love to you because I love you. I love you, Brandon. Mmm, Brandon, Brandon, I love you, ah, I love you, ah, ah, ah, OH!"

This wasn't what I wanted Nicole to say to me, especially not while we were having sex, but I kept going, and she really got into it and worked herself into a shuddering, shaking, squealing, quivering, piston-pumping orgasm, after which I rolled her over and pumped my own piston until there wasn't anything left to pump.

"Brandon," she said happily afterwards.

"Nicole," I said, not at all sure how I felt.

"I love you," she said, clearly hoping that I would say it back this time.

What would have happened if I had said it?

I didn't yet want to admit to myself that I loved Nicole. It was true that we had formed a bond of shared enjoyment, through our companionship and compatibility on multiple levels. Nonetheless, in my head, my narrow definition of "love" made me unwilling to apply that word to Nicole. She didn't seem right for me somehow. Perhaps I was frightened of her. Perhaps being confronted with this situation forced me into a rare moment of considering the future consequences of my actions.

I didn't say it. It wasn't something I was prepared to say just then. And perhaps I was wrong. Maybe I should have told Nicole that I loved her. Maybe the words would have been true on some level. Maybe the act of simply saying the words themselves would have made them truer than they had ever been before. Maybe I could have avoided some serious trouble by saying the words back to her in that moment. Or, maybe my troubles would have been even worse. I don't know. All I know is what I said to her instead.

"Nicole," I said, "you're a wonderful person and I like you a lot, but I'm engaged to another woman."

I know, I know. It wasn't a very tactful thing to say in that moment, right after we had just made love. I admit it. If I'd just left off the bit about the other woman, she probably would have just let it ride; but I'm not always a very tactful person, and I let it slip; and man, did she let me have it.

She began by reminding me of something I had said to her that first evening, while we were out for drinks. It seems I had opened up to Nicole, and related to her some of the issues that I had been having in my relationship with Sarah. Nicole had perhaps taken this to mean that I was potentially working my way around to eventually breaking off my engagement with Sarah, in favor of herself. That wasn't really what I meant, so I suppose I had never clarified this point. Was it an intentional omission? Nah, man, nothing about this was intentional. I had no idea what I was doing. I was just doing shit: I was not thinking about what I did. I don't think I really knew what I wanted.

That was a really ferocious argument, starting in bed with a woman who underwent an instantaneous transformation from a nakedly lustful sex-kitten into a ferocious monster, a man-eating lion, a great goggling gargoyle with outstretched talons and bloodstained teeth. I don't remember everything that was said, nor will I attempt to recall it at this time. It was nasty and unpleasant. What I do remember is that after that night, Nicky didn't invite me over to her house again for a very long time.

But by this time, although I did not want to admit it to myself, I had privately in the back of my mind developed certain feelings for Nicole; and even though I had stopped seeing her very often, those other feelings didn't go away; which really complicated the issue, especially when Nicky started to act all hurt about the whole thing.

*   *   *

I'm noticing that as I relate these events I'm so far really focusing on my relationship with Nicole, with a sideline on my relationship with Becky.   What, one may very well reasonably ask, was going on in my relationship with Sarah all this time?

It's hard to explain in a way that would really make anyone understand. Despite what my relationship with her has become now, I feel that my soul is bound to Sarah's in a way that will last for my entire life, perhaps even longer. What was really stupid is that I was relying too heavily on the knowledge that our connection was eternal and infinite on some level, and thus I wasn't going out of my way to ensure that our connection was maintained in the immediate present. I was bad, I was neglectful. I was an absolute asshole.

But you know, not that it excuses me or anything, but really at least in the beginning Sarah was kind of doing it too, if you see what I mean. We allowed all these unspoken feelings to build up until we got in that argument that one time...

Have I already mentioned that argument with Sarah? I feel like I may have already talked about it, but it stands out in my mind as one of those inconceivably stupid things that people allow to come between them. It was because Sarah and I allowed ourselves to feel separated, for that little slice of our lives, that the separation, once created, was given an opportunity to magnify over time...

I don't even remember what started it, but it ended up involving all kinds of things, until finally Sarah stormed out

72

of the house, and I don't know where she went but she hadn't come back by the time I went to work, and she still wasn't there when I got home late that night, nor was she there when I awoke late the next morning, and I was like, well, what the hell, maybe she's at her Mother's house, but maybe she's having an affair, but even if that's the case, it's okay because we will always love each other. So I sat there and obsessed about Nicole instead of worrying about Sarah; and of course, that was the night that Nicky and I hooked up for the first time. When I did finally stumble home at something like 4:30 am, drunk, Sarah was finally there; but we didn't talk to each other much then, nor was our conversation more than perfunctory the next day, at the zoo. We didn't actually speak to each other again for I don't even know how long, several days at least, maybe a week, maybe even more.

And after that, whenever I had free time or amorous inclinations, instead of seeking out Sarah's company, I called Nicole; because early on, Nicole and I were really excited to hang out with each other, whereas Sarah didn't actually seem to give a fuck whether I was there or not.

I mean, think about what it's like when you're living with somebody. It was really disconcerting, because we'd be in the fucking house together and not saying anything to each other. I mean, after a while we started being civil enough to each other again; but we weren't connecting at all. We watched the goddamn television (she liked cozy murder mysteries); we talked on the phone to other people; we went out and told each other where we were going; we exchanged brief messages about phone calls, groceries, and bills; but we didn't actually fucking talk to each other for the more I think about it, five weeks does not sound unreasonable, in fact if you exclude a few trivial conversations I think we hardly talked for as much as three months. We even went out together with our friends a couple times: and throughout those evenings, we talked to them, not to each other, except when we had to. Even when our friends both left the table for a while and we were left alone, we sat in silence, staring at the grains in the wood, the partially empty glasses, the stains on the tabletop, the ashes and crumpled filters in the ashtray, and the enthusiastically drunk people all around us. We probably flirted with strangers, right there in front of each other, I try not to remember.

It was like that for months. I don't even know how long it was; it felt like forever, and the worst thing about it was that we pretended to each other that nothing had changed. Sarah and I even had sex, a few times during that period, but it was perfunctory: not too memorable, and not too often, either. We were sort of going through the motions with each other, but both knowing that there was something in our minds that affected our feelings towards each other, something that we weren't discussing, weren't sharing, weren't talking about, weren't telling each other; and maybe hers was just trivial, like she was still holding on to a grudge over some stupid argument from months ago; or, maybe she was doing exactly what I was doing. I didn't ask.

In fact, whatever was on Sarah's mind, it probably was just trivial. She had probably just stayed over at her Mom's house that one night, and then met a girlfriend for lunch the next day; but she never told me, either way; and obviously she would have known that I was wondering where the hell she had stayed the night, that night: so it seemed most reasonable for me to assume the worst, in a manner of speaking, although honestly from my perspective, it truly *didn't matter*, at this point, because obviously even if she was having an affair, well as I've been saying all along, I was having an affair too. I didn't particularly care about Sarah's sexual fidelity at the time; it wasn't important. What could ever have made me love her less? Nothing, nothing, nothing could ever make me love her less, even if she hurt me badly, I'd be the pathetic loser with her knife in my guts crying "I love you" to her receding back as I lay bleeding on the floor, should it come to that.

It never came to that. Sarah was the sweetest woman, she would never... In fact, I feel like I am the one who caused most of the pain that I'm feeling now: and, for that matter, most of the pain that everyone else is feeling, too.

But maybe I'm being unjust towards myself. Perhaps I'm afflicted by the Catholic guilt with which I was raised, an automatic assumption of sin, blamefulness and the dire consequences of God's wrath. Beg forgiveness for thy sins, ye imperfect mortals! What if I'm crucifying myself for a guilt that I shared with others? The thought makes me want to cry, but I must force myself to think about it in an attempt to consider all the possibilities, because I really do want to understand what happened, in hopes that this total understanding will allow me to put these feelings behind me and try to do something positive with my life that I've been wasting.

Is that a hopeless cause?

I don't know.

Anyway, the important thing is that even if Sarah shared even just the smallest portion of the responsibility for the problems we had with our relationship, in the end she more than paid her due penance, and in fact she was completely exonerated, for eventually it was she who attempted to re-initiate our previous state of happy companionship.

*   *   *

But that didn't happen for a while. What happened first is that my sleep deprivation continued, I was drinking too much, I wasn't smiling very often, I got all uptight about totally unimportant things and just generally behaved like an unbalanced, paranoid stress case around everybody who spent any time with me.

Nicole, pissed off that I had spurned her offer of love, and still jealous about how well I got along with her roommate Becky, had not asked me over to see her for weeks and weeks. At work, she changed her schedule so that she worked fewer shifts with me, and when we did work together, she didn't talk to me any more than she absolutely had to, which on many evenings was not at all.

So that was that. I wasn't seeing Nicky any more. It was over. I never heard from her, she wasn't talking to me. Our affair seemed to have ended; and, given the potential for fireworks, this ending had entailed thankfully little drama. All in all, it was for the best. I thought I understood: I hadn't been giving Nicky what she wanted from me, and besides, why would she have wanted to be with a fuck-up like me in the first place?

But at the very same time, my relationship with Sarah was sucking so bad, it was practically non-existent. Living together had become totally uncomfortable. We were ignoring each other so convincingly that we even pretended that we weren't ignoring each other. It made me sad to be in the room with her, it made me sad to be in the room when she wasn't home, and somehow even when we spoke together, we couldn't connect, neither of us wanted to or knew how to break down the communication barrier which had grown between us.

Weeks passed. Nicole didn't call me. Sarah never talked to me. I felt alone, so very alone, even though I was surrounded by people, all the time.

Everything was bad. Our town was hit with an incessant deluge of rain, so that the sky was bleak and my clothes were constantly damp for weeks on end. My relationships sucked. I felt terrible. I caught a bad cold, and it lingered, so I went around with a stuffy head, a nasty cough and a hoarse voice for a month or more.

And all the time, I had this horrible premonition that everything would soon get much, much worse.

*   *   *

I allowed myself to develop a mild case of paranoia that focused on Nicole and her attitude towards me. Specifically, I was worried about how intentionally and obviously distant she was acting towards me when I was in her vicinity at work. In front of our co-workers, we had never acted as if we were involved in any kind of relationship; but ever since we had begun spending a lot of time together outside of work, we had at least been generally pretty friendly with each

76

other when we were scheduled to work together. Now she was being cold to me once again, as cold as she had ever been; and you can probably see why that might be alarming to me. Nicole had information that could easily put me in a very precarious position: such as, for example, the information that she and I had engaged in raunchy sexual intercourse on the floor of the restaurant's back office. This information would surely cost me my job, should it be revealed; and I feared to think of what it might do to my relationship with Sarah.

Perhaps the pitiful amount of thought that I put into this last question should be telling. For whatever reason, I was convinced that what I had done did not have to have any effect on the long-term plans that I had been working on, the life which I was attempting to structure. My ongoing relationship with Sarah and my now-concluded affair with Nicole existed in different worlds; they did not need to influence or be affected by each other. I saw no reason why this should change.

First of all, I thought Sarah would never know. I would give her no reason to find out. I felt guilty about this, though, and sometimes considered telling her. I hoped she would understand that no indiscretion on my part could ever change the way I felt about her; that all the things I had ever said to her were as true as ever and would always continue to be true, that I would always love her and could never love anyone else more than I loved her. Those things never stopped being true! Those things have not stopped being true, even now, which is what's really fucking with my head because of what happened, and if I could stop loving her it would be easier, but I will always love her, and that's why I am hurting so bad right now, because of what I did. This isn't what I thought would happen. I never allowed myself to consider this possibility. I put the thought away from me. I didn't think about jack shit. I feared the implications of my actions, but I didn't want to admit to that fear; so I didn't allow myself to spend time thinking about what Sarah would do if she found out.

I didn't want to let myself worry, so I placated my fears with shallow dismissive illusions, and blissfully continued walking blindly through the fog of my life, not even realizing that I couldn't see what was around me. After a while, I almost forgot that there was still something I was trying not to let myself think about.

*   *   *

I had really been missing Sarah, even though I'd been living with her the whole time. Sarah and I had not been getting along, as I've mentioned; and regardless of who was responsible for our communication breakdown, we both felt aggrieved. I'm sure we were both hurting each other, through action or inaction. Our relationship was really falling apart for no good reason, and it felt really hopeless and depressing. While I was having my brief but intense relationship with Nicole, I felt completely cut off from the relationship I had previously enjoyed with Sarah, my fiancée who I loved very deeply; and even though I was busily falling in love with Nicole (and her roommate) it didn't mean that I loved Sarah any less: she remained dear to me, as she always will, and it hurt to feel so separated from her, and maybe that's why it was so easy for me to become so involved with someone else.

But maybe Sarah felt the same feelings of loss and separation from me, and maybe she felt that it was all my fault, and maybe she was right, but she saw that I was too stubborn or too stupid to try to fix the situation, and she decided that the responsibility would therefore have to be hers.

*   *   *

One day, out of the blue, Sarah asked me out on a date, which was strangely formal but sounded kind of silly and fun. It was her subtle way of trying to make things between us be OK again: first by asking me out to dinner, then by drawing me out in conversation. I had been feeling really lonely and isolated; so when my beloved made this proposal, I readily assented.

She insisted that we had to get all dressed up. She wore this dress that on another woman might have been kind of plain, but on her it was so very sexy that I couldn't stop looking at her body, the whole time we were sitting across from each other at the table.

We went to some fancy Italian restaurant, and ordered expensive food and a bottle of wine, and as we sat there, we toasted each other and smiled, and it felt good to be together for the first time in maybe months. And Sarah struck up a conversation with me, and we talked for a while, looking into each other's eyes; and we started to get excited about whatever it was we were talking about, until we were talking once again in the familiar manner of good friends and lovers who have known each other throughout the years.

Sarah and I laughed and joked and flirted, and it was almost as exciting to be with her that night as it had been the first time we met, years and years ago. Our fingertips and legs sought surreptitious contact with each other under the table, and we smiled into each other's eyes as we told recent stories from work and old tales from our childhoods. In that moment all the negative energy which had existed between us for so long simply evaporated, as we drank another glass of wine and ate some tasty food and chatted each other up one side and down the other.

We left the restaurant, giddy with wine and our rediscovered romantic connection. Then we went home and made the sweetest love you could ever imagine. That night, it was special. That night, Sarah and I made ten-point perfect love together. We'd had a lot of practice with each other, over the years, so we were comfortably familiar with each other's bodies; yet we were still exciting and mysterious to each other, and that night was the first time in a while: so we both surrendered to each other, smooth, darkly seductive, talking in husky voices, filling each other's minds and senses with love, love, love.

It felt insurpassably wonderful to be together. That night, we both believed that everything would be OK, forever.

*   *   *

That was the night when everything changed again. That night, I really thought that life could have maybe gone back to being the way I used to think I wanted it to be, before all this started. That was the night when my relationship with Sarah finally began to improve, following a long period of unpleasant stagnation.

And after that night, everything really seemed to be better, for a while. For a while, I really thought that everything was all right.

After that night, Sarah and I suddenly found time for each other again. We stole moments to giggle and snuggle together, to bake cookies together; we woke each other up in the middle of the night to make love.

In the time that followed, my relationship with Sarah once again became my focus, my properly overriding concern, and the fact that Nicky never called me didn't really bother me any more. At work, she continued to more or less ignore me for a while, but still she was generally more or less civil, usually, so in time I succeeded in forgetting about it. My affair with Nicky had clearly ended, and even if our continued association wasn't quite as friendly as I would have liked, still, as these things go, it hadn't been a real painful or even specifically agreed-upon break-up. Furthermore, I was relieved to find that the whole thing had concluded without affecting my relationship with Sarah in any way. I had returned to being a good boyfriend. I was no longer involved in any sort of inappropriate behavior. I thought I had nothing to fear.

For a while, everything seemed so much better.

*   *   *

I'm trying to remember which came next. Was it the talk I had with Nicky at work? Or was it the time I ran into Becky at the bookstore?

I'll tell you about my talk with Nicole first because I think it came first, maybe two weeks after my joyful reunion with my beloved Sarah. As I've mentioned, Nicole hadn't been calling me for a while before I got back together with Sarah; and then, after Sarah and I went on our date and rediscovered our bond, time continued to pass and Nicole continued to not call me. But by then I wasn't too worried about Nicky, because by then I was getting along with Sarah so well again. Sure, Nicky was a little snooty to me at work sometimes, when she wasn't completely ignoring me; but frankly that was how we'd started off, so even though it disturbed me a bit, I tried not to let it.

Then finally one day at work it all came down.

It began with one of those really dumb arguments that started off as something stupid, a misunderstanding, somebody taking something the wrong way, possibly on purpose. In fact I actually think it really started when I said something polite and generic like "How are you doing?" But I looked at her and smiled as I said it, to indicate that I still felt close to her in a secret way, so she wouldn't think that I totally took her for granted or something. As it turned out, though, that was what she claimed to feel.

"As if you cared," she said, or something like it, except I don't think her statement was that concise; what she said was something more like "I don't believe that you give a rat's ass how I am, or what I'm feeling, or whether or not I'm even alive, you selfish prick."

"Whoah, Nicky, don't say that," I said, looking around to see if anyone was within hearing distance. "It's totally not true, I like you a lot. What's bothering you?"

"You totally used me," she said. "You came over and hung out all the time for a while and we had a great time together, and then you just sort of never showed up again, no explanation, you just never called-"

"I thought," I interrupted, "it seemed to me that you had stopped inviting me over."

"Well," she snapped, "I didn't want to be just, like, throwing myself at you or something, if it wasn't something that you were interested in."

"I really enjoy your company. I told you so. What do you want from me?" I said, but just then somebody else came in, one of the other wait staff, who was on that night? I don't remember; probably Jasmine, I think that for whatever reason, if Nicole and I ever did anything implicating ourselves while we were at work, then Jasmine would have been the one to witness it, that poor girl ended up seeing all kinds of shit she didn't want to see, like that one fight, but that was later on. As it was, after Jasmine came into the kitchen, Nicole and I just acted like we had been discussing business, then we went back to filling orders. A few minutes later, back out on the floor, I passed by her and paused long enough to say, "Talk to you after work?" She nodded and we went back to what we had been doing.

So then after work that night, after the rest of the staff left, Nicole and I had the predictable argument, out on the floor in between the tables with the chairs up on top of them, legs up in the air like a denuded forest.

She said again that I had used her. I said I'd never been anything but honest with her. She said I'd been disrespectful by ignoring her of late. I said I had thought she wanted it that way. She claimed that I had never asked. I said, "Well, I'm here now, so why don't you tell me. What is it that you want?" She just gave me some line of shit like, "I just want you to respect me and treat me as an equal," to which I said, of course, that's what I always do, and she lit into me about how callous and unsympathetic, uncaring and unconcerned it was of me to ignore her for the past few weeks, after getting along with her so well for a while, and how could I claim that I treated her with respect, when I was allowing her to feel so abandoned by me.

It was a little too intense, with the abandonment accusations and everything. These weren't the things I wanted to hear from Nicole; but I was afraid that she was right. I was afraid that I had been less than gentlemanly in my treatment of her as a lover; and this disturbed me, because I honestly would never have wanted any of my lovers to get out of a relationship with me feeling that I had treated them poorly. I didn't want Nicole to feel harshly spurned. But that gentleness was my downfall.

Don't get me wrong. I didn't just go back to her place that night because I felt sorry for her or something. No, I genuinely liked Nicole. She was a very attractive young woman, and we seemed to get along well when we spent time together. I see now that she took advantage of this to maneuver me into a disadvantageous position. But at the time she didn't seem to have any ulterior motives other than the basic need to feel loved and important to somebody.

And the fact of the matter is that I had grown to love Nicole. I didn't think of it that way; I certainly never said anything like that to her, even when she clearly wanted me to; and although I loved her in my own way, I would not say that I was really "in love" with her, especially. Yet love her I did. You may scoff, but I mean it sincerely. What other word is there for the warm feelings of fondness that I felt for Nicole? My emotional attachment to her went beyond the purely sexual. She had been there for me when I was having problems in my relationship with Sarah. Nicole had been sweet, kind, sympathetic, and entertaining. She helped me to forget about my problems and focus my energy on the joy of being alive; which helped me to exude the kind of happy vibes that made it easier to fix my problems with Sarah. Does that twisted logic make sense, that by loving Nicole I was able to love Sarah more? It sounds stupid when I say it out loud, but that was how I felt at the time. And I felt gratitude to Nicky for that; and when I saw her feeling sad, lonely and rejected, I wanted to give her back some of the happy vibes that she had given me.

So I went home with Nicole that one last time. I wonder if she and I both knew without discussing it that it would be the last time. I'm sure we both suspected that it would be, because Nicky and I had not formed a really solid basis to our relationship, and we had allowed time, space and miscommunication to make us feel distant from and maybe even antagonistic towards each other. One night of shagging could never be enough to overcome the weeks which had preceded it, during which neither of us had called the other, and apparently both felt neglected as a result.

But I guess we felt that we had to try, at least; so I went home with her after work and made sweet love to her, with all the tenderness and gentle caresses that I could muster. I pleasured her body with all the tricks I could think of, I moved with her to try to get to all the secret deep sensitive spots, she moaned and laughed and she cried too, and I laughed with her and kissed away her tears until we came together and it felt like we had achieved a wonderful connection to each other, a union that could not be explained in conventional terms. We snuggled in silence for a while afterward, then nuzzled each other and kissed, and talked in hushed conspiratorial voices. Then I fell asleep.

My relationship with Sarah could have been ended by that incident alone, if things had gone differently: but I guess, all things considered, I am one lucky son of a bitch. I woke up only a few minutes after falling asleep, and realized the precarious nature of my position. If I slept the whole night through with Nicole, then Sarah would know exactly what had happened, and I would be in serious trouble. I kissed Nicole's forehead and extracted myself from the snuggle position we had been in. She woke up and watched me get dressed. When I had my clothes on, I sat down on the edge of the bed and stroked her cheek and hair with my fingers.

"It was good to see you," I said.

She turned away and buried her face in her pillow.

"I hope you sleep well and have pleasant dreams," I told her.

She looked back up at me. "I don't want you to go," she said.

"I'm sorry," I said, "I have to."

"You're a bastard," she informed me, "and I'm gonna miss you."

"Oh, Nicole, Nicole," I whispered, and crawled back under the blankets to give her a big hug. She gave me a couple of wet kisses and buried her face in my shoulder. I held her until her breathing slowed, then once again extracted myself from the snuggle and stepped quietly out of the room.

I walked quietly, a few steps down the hallway, around the corner past the kitchen, and into the living room with the TV and the couches and the front door. I had nearly reached the front door when I heard keys jingling from outside. As I stood there in front of the door, it opened, and in stepped brunette Becky. I had to take a step back just to avoid being hit by the door.

The porch light was on. The living room was dark.

"Hi, Becky," I said.

Becky gave a small shriek, and accused me of hiding in the dark.

"I was just on my way home," I explained.

"Well, that's too bad," Becky said with a flirtatious smile, and I could smell alcohol on her breath, "because I just got here."

"Well, I'm glad you got here before I left instead of afterwards," I told her truthfully. "It's good to see you, you're looking good." And indeed she was looking really, truly fine that evening: she was dressed to kill, actually, and if she had wanted to bring a man home, she surely would have had one with her; but here she was, alone, smiling at me.

"Are you sure you have to go now?" she said.

"I, what time is it?" I said. She told me. "Yeah, I should probably go."

"Your loss," she said; and I thought, *What the hell, today is my lucky day.* I moved in close and slid my arms around Becky's waist. She gave me a big hug, and then we kissed.

"It's too bad," I said in her ear, "that I never get to see you alone, Becky."

"Yeah," she agreed, speaking into my neck, her hands on my back, holding me tight.

"Maybe we should hang out sometime?" I suggested.

"I'd like that," she told me, thrilling me with the soft tones of her raspy alto voice.

"Would you?" I asked.

"Yeah." We kissed again, more sensuously this time. Then Becky said, "Except that you're sleeping with my roommate."

I pulled back a little. "I cannot claim innocence," I mumbled, looking her in the eye only briefly before averting my gaze to the floor.

"Well," she said, "so Nicole probably wouldn't like it if we started hanging out."

"She might be upset," I agreed, thinking of the tears of jealousy that Nicole was already crying.

"That's a problem," said Becky.

She doesn't want to hang out with me, I thought, *and that's fine. The moral issues involved here are insurmountable. I should not have made the attempt. I should just say goodnight and leave.*

But then Becky continued. "So I guess," she said with a wicked smile, "that means we'll have to find some time when she's not around."

I nearly laughed out loud, and would have if I hadn't been afraid that Nicole would hear. "I can't believe you just said that," I told her. "That's so bad. And you seem like such a nice person!"

She grinned and stood up on her toes. "Well, what else am I supposed to do?" she said, and we kissed once more. Her tongue explored my mouth, my lips sucked on her lips, we pressed our bodies together, I grabbed her ass and pushed her up against the wall but then she shoved me away and said, "I want to have coffee with you sometime. We'll talk and get to know each other."

"Okay," I said lamely.

"Should I give you a call?" she pressed, so I gave her my cell phone number and told her to leave me a message if I didn't pick up.

It was really late when I got home that night, and I didn't even have an excuse cooked up: but like I said before, I was one lucky son of a bitch. Sarah didn't even stir when I climbed into bed next to her. I thought happily of how wonderful she was, and how lucky I was to be in bed with her. I smiled at my unprecedented success with women in these past few months. I hoped that Nicole would not feel too hurt; I hoped that I would get to see Becky again soon; and I hoped that Sarah would love me forever.

And I tried not to allow myself to be bothered by the contradiction.

*   *   *

So I guess after that a couple of weeks had passed, and Becky had not called me, and I had reached the conclusion that despite whatever she had said to me that one night while she was drunk and horny, Becky would never actually call me in the sober light of day; and that was okay. In the meantime, Nicole had not called me, either; but that was okay, too, because when I saw her at work, she would sometimes smile at me, and I was nice to her, even invited her to call me sometime, but she didn't, so I figured that she was trying to move on with her life, and you know, I couldn't blame her.

So like I'm saying, I hadn't heard from either of them in a while, maybe two weeks, but it was all OK, because like I said, after a period of time when we hadn't been talking much, I was once again really enjoying the time I spent with Sarah: and I was really glad, and I should have just left well enough alone at that point.

*   *   *

I was at a book store, thinking about getting a gift for Sarah, actually, when who should walk around the corner and down my aisle but little brunette Becky, browsing for books. I spotted her first, and I immediately thought with a pang of our last interaction.

I want to stop being unfaithful to Sarah, I thought to myself, *because she is such a wonderful woman and I would never want to hurt her.*

Becky saw me then, as I was thinking of Sarah, and she said, "Hi," but she didn't smile. I supposed that she too was thinking of our last encounter, and of the suggestive potentials we had filled it with; and I supposed that she too was no longer sure it was something she still wanted.

"Howdy," I said. "Are you looking for some books?" What a stupid question. All around us, densely packed on rows and rows of shelves that towered over our heads, arranged alphabetically by author, were books of every description, new, used, good, awful. I guess she was okay with the inanity of my conversation, though; maybe because she was relieved that the first words out of my mouth hadn't been, "coffee together." So we talked about books for a while, and gradually warmed to the subject when we found that we had read and enjoyed a number of the same ones. The discussion grew more intriguing, lively and exciting, until eventually I actually bought one on her recommendation; after which we walked together to a coffee shop, ordered some caffeine and sat down at a table, almost as if we had planned the whole thing.

Becky and I did not have sex that day; nor did we have sex the next time we met, again for coffee, a few days later. No, we did something much more dangerous: we got to know each other. We found that we had so much in common, we seemed to have known each other for a long time, and we quickly opened up to each other with all kinds of deeply personal information that one doesn't usually share with other people. We discussed everything from spirituality and physics to ethics, environmentalism, history, anthropology, comparative religions, psychology, literature: our conversations were like a whole liberal arts education. Our talks were exciting; we both got all worked up, and looked each other in the eyes as we sat close together, our bodies touching, our faces so close that we occasionally bumped noses. We speculated on the possibility of a cosmic plan that had intentionally brought us together, to teach each other about life and the world. We rediscovered, explored and strengthened the incredibly powerful bond which had instantaneously formed between us, months previously during our sexy drunken love triangle with Nicole; for, we both agreed, in later discussions, that in the first moment when I had first entered Becky on that crazy night, our contact was so intense that it transcended the mere sexual, as if we were no longer experiencing our bodies as solid matter, but as though we had become vehicles for the blissful mingling of the cosmic energy of the universe itself.

In the process of our soul-baring conversations, I felt compelled to confess to Becky that I was engaged to Sarah, and that I had been cheating on Sarah with Nicole and, on one occasion, with Becky herself. At the time, Becky didn't really react to this reference to our single unusual encounter, but instead she asked me perceptive and nonjudgmental questions about my relationships with the two other women, how I felt about them and what I wanted to see happen. I told her that I was no longer sure if I wanted what I had always thought I wanted, and left it at that.

Up until just a few minutes before, I had been convinced that I could never love anyone the way I loved Sarah. Suddenly, talking to Becky, I felt my potentials multiply, when I realized that I could love her, too, perhaps just as deeply. I didn't tell her that, exactly; but I think she knew that was what I meant. We were quiet for a little while, thinking; and then she asked me if I would like to meet her in private sometime, and I said yes.

*   *   *

I was already in a bad mood on the day I got the call. My bicycle had gotten a flat tire on the way to work, and I had to walk it for the last mile and a half, so that I was very late for my shift. My boss snapped at me on his way out, for making him stay late; and I got a withering look from Justin the dishwasher, who I had reprimanded for a lesser tardiness only the previous day. I was trying to catch up with my day's duties in the face of a barrage of impatient customers, when my cell phone rang. I had forgotten to switch it off, another offense for which I had been known to chastise employees on a number of occasions. I moved back into the office, silenced the ringer and sent the call to voicemail, and then switched off the phone; but not before my caller ID informed me that the call I'd just missed had been from Nicole's cell phone. It was the first time she'd called me in weeks; the first time since the last time we'd made love: our farewell fuck, as it were.

I did not think much of it at the time, and returned to work. Several hours later when I finally got a break, I checked my voicemail.

"Please enter your password," said the recording.

I pressed some numbers on the phone.

"You have one unheard message," said the machine. "First message:"

Then Nicole's voice came on. Speaking in a quiet, restrained, obviously upset voice, she said, "Hi, Brandon, it's Nicole, how are you? Listen, there's something we need to talk about, uh, something's come up and I have to talk to you, so give me a call as soon as you can, okay? Thanks, bye."

My mind reeled. I felt as if I'd just been struck by a speeding truck. The way I saw it, her message could only mean one thing, and it was the very last thing that I wanted just then.

After my first two thoughtless sexual encounters with Nicole, I had finally asked her about birth control, and she had assured me that she was taking the pill. Now, it was a bit of an assumption, but if I understood her message correctly, that method had apparently failed.

Nicole was pregnant.

I called her back.

"Can you come over?" was the first thing she said.

"I'll be there after work," I assured her.

When I arrived, Nicole was alone; Becky was thankfully absent.

In a few short words, Nicole confirmed my worst fears.

"I'm three weeks late," she told me, "so I went to a the doctor today, and..."

"Was it me?" I asked.

She gave me a you're-such-a-fucking-asshole glare and said, "I haven't been with anyone else for a long time."

"What happened?" I asked. "I thought you were on the pill."

"I was, Brandon, but just before I had sex with you that last time, I missed a few days. Then the day after, I took a whole bunch of them, but apparently it didn't work. I'm really sorry."

I fought back the urge to accuse her of getting pregnant on purpose. "You didn't do it on purpose," I said instead. "I'm sorry, too, Nicole," I went on. "It's really unfortunate, because it's not at all what I would have wanted to happen right now."

"I know it's bad timing, Brandon, but I want to... I don't want to have an-" and her words broke down into sobs as tears streamed down her face.

I took her in my arms, and she collapsed sobbing against me. "Oh, Nicole, I'm so sorry," I said, still fighting back the angry suspicion that this whole scene was being choreographed. "But please don't have it," I said. "Neither of us is in the right life situation for a baby right now. I can't imagine becoming a father at this phase of my life," I told her. "It's too soon." *And,* I didn't say, *you aren't the woman I want to marry and raise children with, anyway.*

Nicole pushed me away. "You're so fucking selfish!" she screamed at me through her tears. "You think it's all about you! How do you think *I* feel, have you ever considered that, Brandon? How do you think this makes me feel?"

"Please, Nicole, try to stay calm."

"Fuck you!" she screamed.

"Okay, how does it make you feel?" I asked her in the most sympathetic tone I could muster through the rage that was struggling to burst out of my eyeballs and eardrums. "Come on, tell me about it."

Suddenly she wasn't screaming any more. "I feel like dirt," she sobbed. "I feel like the worst thing that ever crawled on the face of the earth. I want to go find a corner and die. I fucked up, and I know it, I didn't want it to be like this, but now I feel like maybe this was meant to happen, and maybe it's my opportunity to do the right thing for once." She turned her pleading, imploring, bloodshot eyes to mine.

"Nicole," I said, "I know you think I'm being selfish, but really I'm thinking of you, too. Look at where you are with your life, and try to imagine raising a kid. You don't make much money as it is, and your baby would take up all of your time. You'd be stuck doing what you're doing, you'd never really be able to move on with your life. It would be so much harder for you to go back to school, or to be a model, like you said you wanted to be; Nicole, you're beautiful, you'd be a great model, but it would be harder for you to get in with stretch marks and matronly breasts."

She laughed, briefly, then cried harder. She allowed me to hold her again, and I felt so sad and upset that I soon found that I was crying, too. We held each other and pressed our wet cheeks together until she kissed me.

We didn't know what else to do, so we made love. She continued crying, through a lot of it, but she was no less enthusiastic for all her tears. Afterwards, as we held each other on Nicole's bed, we discussed the issue at length. Though we argued, we didn't raise our voices again. Much of the time we were both laying on our backs, side by side, our fingers clasped, looking at the ceiling and talking in intimate tones.

After our argument had gone back and forth many times, Nicky finally said what was on her mind.

"Can you imagine trying to raise a kid by yourself?" I had just asked her. "You don't want to be a single mother."

"You could marry me," she answered. I looked at her. She was looking at the ceiling, her face expressionless.

I put my hand on her belly. "Nicole," I said, "I like you a lot, and I'm really glad that I've had the chance to get to know you, but I don't think you and I are meant to be together, do you? I mean, I think if we were forced into a permanent relationship because of this, we would resent each other, we'd end up feeling trapped. We'd kill each other! I really don't think it's a good idea."

Nicole removed my hand from her belly. "Fuck you, Brandon," she said.

I kissed her cheek.

"No, I mean it," she said, "you're a fucking asshole."

"Sweetie, don't be like that," I said. It was the first time I had ever called her 'sweetie.'

"I feel like you totally used me," she said, not for the first time. "I was your toy while it was convenient for you, and now you think you should be able to just discard me and forget about me. I feel like I was never important to you, and it hurts, Brandon, it makes me feel really bad, because you're important to me."

I had never thought of the relationship in those terms. I felt terrible that I could have made Nicky feel so bad, but I refused to accept her interpretation.

"Of course you are important to me, Nicky," I said. "I've had a lot of fun with you, and I think you're a great person, and I care for you, I really do." I had never formulated these words to this girl; they felt awkward, and consequently I vastly understated the case. I was totally uncomfortable, but I knew that I had to keep going. "I'm really sorry that I made you feel bad," I said. "I truly didn't mean to. I thought you understood; I thought we both saw it the same way."

"Maybe at first, Brandon, but not after a while; after a while I start to get attached. I can't help it, it's just the way I am."

"But do you see?" I persisted. "Don't you agree that we would kill each other?"

Nicole shook her head and looked away.

"I mean, look at us!" I said, as if this proved anything.

Nicole was silent for a long time, then she said, "I suppose it's the sort of thing that would only work if we both wanted it. I think we could be really good together, and I'm sorry you don't see it the same way."

I tried to find a way to placate her: "But we are really good together; I just don't think we'd work... like *that*."

She ignored my words. "Sometimes I have dreams about you," she said, "dreams where you tell me the things I want to hear from you; but then when I wake up in the morning, I know that it was just a dream, and you'll only ever say those things to me inside my own head. I feel like your soul is a part of my soul, Brandon, but you've chosen to be cut off from that recognition. It makes me so angry that sometimes I didn't call you for weeks, just out of the hopes that you would call me; and after a while, you didn't call me any more, and I felt like I was losing part of my life, part of my soul. Then you came over that last time, but it wasn't what I wanted from you at all. I realized that night that you've closed off the possibilities in your mind, and you'd only ever be willing to share a part of yourself with me." She was looking at the ceiling, speaking in a low voice, not touching me. With difficulty, I refrained from cracking a joke about the particular part of my anatomy that I had shared with her. "You think it's all about sex, Brandon, but it's not," Nicole reprimanded me, as though reading my thoughts. "Sex is an expression of love, even if you don't mean it to be; and if you express that love enough, even with someone you don't think you feel that way about... it *creates* those feelings, and strengthens them, and forms a bond." She turned to look at me, then. "I will always love you, Brandon," she said. "You are an important part of my life and I will never forget you. And now there's a life inside of me that's a part of my life, and it's a part of your life too."

I was crushed. The litany of my sins was multiplying before my eyes. I had made all the wrong choices in so many ways, I couldn't even begin to count them all. I had hurt Nicole, unintentionally, but in a very real and painful way, through carelessness and misunderstandings, and here I was, still hurting her.

I apologized again, but I knew that the word "sorry" was pathetically insufficient, it was but a mist blowing off the ocean of right and wrong. "I feel terrible," I told Nicole, "I honestly never meant to make you feel bad, and I certainly never intended this to happen."

"I didn't intend it, either, Brandon. You probably think I got pregnant on purpose, to try to trap you into a relationship with me or something, because you really are that paranoid, and everybody knows it. But it's not like that. I was just really depressed, I genuinely forgot to take those pills and I didn't even realize it until the next day. But Brandon," she continued, "I want to have this child." I could tell that she was struggling to not cry. "I can already feel the changes in my body, and it feels so right, everything about me is telling me to keep it. If I don't have it, I will be going against the whole purpose of my being. But I don't want to do it by myself. I'm scared, Brandon, I'm scared."

With that, the dam broke, and the tears she'd been holding back burst forth in a torrential flood. I pulled her to me, wrapped my arms around her, held her close, but felt miles away. I wasn't prepared to cope with all the life-shattering information that was pounding on the inside of my skull. Seeing myself through Nicky's eyes made me feel so utterly degraded that I tried to shut myself off and go through the motions of what I felt I should do, in the detached manner of a robot operated by remote control. The fear that she might have my child was threatening to devastate my life as I knew it. What I was feeling inside was so intense that I didn't know what to do with it all; so I turned away, intellectually. I tried to slam the door on my feelings and immerse myself in the escapism of non-participation.

I was frightened by my feelings in this moment because mingled amongst them was one whose presence I hadn't suspected: an intruder, as it were; but I realized that this intruder feeling had been comfortably situated inside my reality for a long time, and whether it stayed firmly rooted in my subconscious, or whether I scorched and twisted my inner world in an effort to evict it: either way it would leave a permanent mark; either way it was a factor in my life that I would have to deal with. I didn't want to deal with it.

I was suddenly petrified with the fear that I loved Nicole, after all.

I had never allowed myself to think of her that way. The one night where she'd said the words to me, I had been almost repulsed by the thought; love between us did not fit into my tidily ordered plans for my life. But this night, as we made love to the accompaniment of the sound of her weeping, I had, just briefly, looked into her eyes, and she had looked into mine, and in that moment I felt the connection that I had been shunning. Unbidden, the words arose in my mind: *I love you.* I didn't say them. I couldn't say them. I didn't want what they implied. I had already made my decisions and these words didn't have a place there. But I thought them, all the same: I love you, Nicole. As I looked into her eyes, I knew she was thinking the same thing about me, although for her, that love was already mingled with love's closest companion, hatred.

Accompanying this unwanted discovery of my love for Nicole was the realization that I had felt it before. I remembered similar experiences on previous occasions, during our lovemaking sessions and the glow that followed, when the same words had presented themselves to my attention: I love you, Nicole. At the time, I had misunderstood the nature of love so completely that I didn't actually believe that they could be true, so I had chosen not to say them then. Now, as I was beginning to realize just how wrong I had been, that the complexities of life don't always fit into the nice orderly plans we make for it: now it was too late, I could never bring myself to say them. I had already said too many contradictory words; I had already made too many decisions that rendered love futile. In my mind, all my plans were still for Sarah.

So we talked and argued late into the night, and she poured forth tears and accusations, and I responded to her from my vantage point on a far distant lofty precipice, the solitary peak from which I was observing our conversation.

We hadn't really decided anything by the time I left.

As I drove home, I felt like dirt. I felt like the worst thing that had ever crawled on the face of the earth. I wanted to find a corner and die there.

I had fucked up, and I knew it.

*   *   *

I remained perched on my lofty precipice for the next couple of weeks. I was detached from everything in my life, I didn't really connect with any people or experiences, I didn't participate in the great mystery of life: instead, I withdrew.

After several more long uncomfortable discussions, Nicole finally agreed to have a procedure done. I drove her to the clinic and paid for it. She had offered to split it with me, but I said, "This is the least I can do."

She cried all the way home, after it was done. I didn't know what to say to her, and she was turned away from me, looking out the window, an expression of tear-streaked emotional agony convoluting the features of her face. "It hurt," was all she said. "It was really painful. They were tearing out a part of me."

I reached over and put a hand on her knee. She didn't acknowledge it. Soon afterwards, I went around a corner, and needed both hands for the steering wheel; I didn't put my hand back on her knee, after that.

In the days that followed, Nicky didn't call me, and I didn't call her. The days stretched into weeks and I began to return from my emotional distance, but she and I hardly looked at each other when I saw her at work. I didn't know what to say to her; and she'd said everything she wanted to say to me. I started to feel that she would be happier if she didn't have to interact with me at all; so I tried to remove myself from her sphere of awareness as much as possible.

*   *   *

I soon found that giving Nicole plenty of space was not the cure for the ailment between us. She started acting not just distant but sometimes antagonistic and really rude to me, kind of disdainful and cold, when I saw her at work, until finally one day, I felt that it was getting to be too uncomfortable and wanted to know if there was something I could do to make it better.

I started to ask her what was the matter but she cut me off and told me bluntly that she didn't want to be involved with me any more. I hadn't actually seen her in a while, so didn't see why it was crucial to discuss it right then. I looked around, we were in the kitchen, there were other people working not at all far away, Jasmine was standing right bloody next to me. "Do you want to talk about this later?" I asked as quietly as I could, trying to indicate to her that our conversation would be overheard if we had it now.

"No, I don't want to meet you after work!" she shouted at me. All around the kitchen, heads turned. Out on the floor in the dining area, conversations at the tables suddenly hushed while people listened intently to the words Nicole hurled at me like bricks. It seemed to go on forever. "You never cared about me, you were just using me." Should I grab her and drag her out the back door so the customers wouldn't hear? Would one of the cooks hold me at knifepoint if I tried to touch her? I was frozen with indecision. She continued on with the by now familiar litany of my crimes as I hung my head to avoid the stares of my co-workers, then asked her once again if we could talk about this at a better time. "I don't have time to talk to you later," she said, "because I'm meeting with Randy, and he really cares about me, he and I are true soulmates, he may be my life partner and it's more important for me to be with him than it is to waste my time having pointless discussions with you. There's nothing to talk about, you and I are finished!"

And with that, she walked out onto the floor. Shaken, I tried to figure out what I had come into the kitchen to do, trying to finish whatever mundane task I'd been in the middle of, despite the monstrous incident that had occurred while I was trying to carry it out.

From all the way across the room, the dishwasher squirted me with the dishwashing hose.

"Cut that shit out!" I said, and tried to be so customer-service oriented for the rest of the evening that none of my co-workers would have a chance to speak to me.

*　　*　　*

I think I must be insane. Right? I mean, why the fuck else would I be sitting here in the middle of the goddamned night, writing out the disturbing details of my unethical life story? I'm obsessed, I'm an insomniac, I'm compulsive, I'm addicted, I can't focus on anything and I don't function well in society. I seem to fuck up everything I do and worst of all it's always my fault for doing something stupid and totally avoidable.

You know, here's what's even worse than all that. I still haven't changed my mind. I still believe in a possible state of relationships where people can love each other freely without causing each other pain or suffering from jealousy or insecurity. And by "love" I don't just mean sexual love. No really, I honestly think, in fact I know because I've done it, that it is possible to love, to really deeply love, more than one person at the same time. Why is that wrong? Okay I know the way I went about it was wrong because it was dishonest and caused too much pain; but in general doesn't it seem logical that by passing love around you create more love in the world and the world becomes a better place because of it?

Doesn't fucking matter, dumbass. Maybe it's hypothetically possible, but I sure couldn't make it work.

I guess what I've been trying to not say but hoping to infer by tossing the word "Love" around so much, is that, although I wouldn't have wanted to admit that I loved Nicole, the fact of the matter is, I did. It was difficult for me to come to this realization and it's really only hit me recently; I still don't want to admit it, really, but that doesn't stop it from being true.

It's like this: you don't necessarily have to love somebody to have really great sex with them; but after you have a lot of really great sex with a person, after a while you tend to develop these feelings of love for them.

That statement oversimplifies the situation and puts too much emphasis on fucking. That had a lot to do with it; but there were a number of other, perhaps equally important, factors involved. Nicole and I spent some really quality time together and felt like good friends as well as lovers. We came to understand each other's moods and habits. We ate together. We told each other stories from childhood. We talked until we couldn't think of anything more to say, and then sometimes we sat in comfortable quietness for hours, watching movies.

The thing about love is that it's so closely connected in people's hearts to the other powerful emotions like anger that sometimes you get along better if you really don't love each other.

Nicole and I had started to feel these feelings, but neither of us wanted to admit it. Actually, that's not true: she had wanted to admit it, at one point; she had said it to me, but I wouldn't listen, wouldn't say it back, wasn't willing to believe it about myself, so I was cold to her, maybe, and that's why she blew me off; and I'm not talking about a blow job, either: nah, man, I'm talking about serious harshness at a high volume in a compromising setting.

So there. I loved Nicole. I fucking said it. I think she loved me too. I know she did. She said so, and I know she was telling the truth. We felt a connection to each other that neither of us had wanted in the first place, and it hurt, so we hurt each other, me without meaning to, really, and her, well, at the end, she pretty much damn well did it on purpose now didn't she? She took her revenge... but of course I'm sure I deserved it, every bitter drop.

So after she broke up with me in public like that, well, those feelings of love which I was not yet prepared to admit quickly turned into other strong emotions like rage and sorrow. All rejection is painful, and to be rejected in such a painful way by somebody for whom my tender feelings were still blossoming, it hurt, it made me want to scream cry bang my fucking head against a wall. But I couldn't do these things at home when Sarah was there. I had to wait.

And in the meantime, my thoughts resumed that spiral pattern I told you about earlier, remember, when I first became infatuated with Nicky and I couldn't stop thinking about her and my brain just kept presenting me with those tantalizing erotic images of her, over and over; well now my brain just kept pouring more sadness into my soul, over and over, all day every day for I don't even want to speculate how long, for fuck's sake it's doing it still. Excerpts from the scene in the Wooden Spoon's kitchen when she told me off replayed in my mind on repeat; I imagined her with her new lover, saying disparaging things about me; and I imagined what I would say to her if she called, give her a piece of my mind, but of course she never called. Every few minutes my brain would remind me that she still hadn't called, it would provide me with regular updates on exactly how long it had been since I had last spoken with her. I will admit that once or twice I actually considered calling her, ostensibly to give her a piece of my mind, but thankfully I was able to maintain my will power, because I knew that if I called her, it would be an act of shredding the last few remaining scraps of my self-esteem.

So there I was, caught once again in as they say the downward spiral. That was only the beginning. As events go it was more of a non-event because after the scene in the kitchen at work, the only things that happened were in my head; the rest of the world was crawling by soooooo slooooow, but inside my mind everything was speeding, superfast, jittery and screaming, skidding out of control on the corners. I was sad to have lost Nicole so harshly, I had come to like her a lot, even if I hadn't been spending a lot of time with her lately; to be told that it was no longer an option at all at all at all at all, I felt so cut off it was like a part of me had been physically removed, something inside had been torn and ripped out, leaving me empty and in pain.

*   *   *

I didn't want to let myself love Nicole because I didn't want to end up in the long-term relationship with her that I thought those feelings would automatically imply. I saw Nicole as too volatile, too emotional and unpredictable. She lacked the dependable stability of someone like Sarah.

Her roommate Becky on the other hand, despite the wrongness of the situation, I had known from our first meeting that I would have a great deal of trouble in only relating to her as a merely casual acquaintance, that it would be difficult for me to treat her as just a friend, because something about her eyes, when she looked at me, cut through all my layers of bullshit, all the defenses and posturing that I use to separate myself from the world: Becky saw through all that, into the person I really am, and when she accepted me for who I am, the joy that I felt as a result was nothing short of ecstasy. When I talked to her or spent time around her she excited a deep part of my psyche and effortlessly evoked the same feelings that I had been trying to suppress in my relationship with Nicole, with the difference that I never wanted to repress them or hide them from Becky; I knew I could love her, I wanted to love her, I wanted to let that love blossom and unfold like the jewel of the lotus flower.

I knew it wouldn't be tactful to say things like that to her, in those words, at first; but she had hinted, in our brief conversations, that she felt a similar reaction to me. We were getting along well, and when we saw each other, we felt a spark of connection that soon kindled the raging flames of desire. When last I'd seen her, I had agreed to meet Becky in private sometime; but shortly afterward, Nicole's pregnancy had complicated my life so much that I really didn't feel up to it. So I hadn't called her since that meeting. Becky had e-mailed me once, to tell me that she was going out of town briefly; but she didn't call me when she got back. I don't know if she knew about the abortion; I never told her, but I have to assume that Nicole did. In all the time I knew her, Becky never mentioned it to me.

Time passed. By the time I returned from the fit of depression that the painful ending of my affair with Nicole had precipitated, I had lost my hopes that Becky and I would ever consummate our intended liaison. It didn't seem to fit the picture any more. Nonetheless I continued to cherish a secret unmentionable desire for her, far away in the distant background of my mind, even as I engaged in romantic evenings with Sarah my lovely fiancée.

*   *   *

One day someone e-mailed me a political petition, one of those things where you sign your name at the end and forward it to everyone you know, with the intention that the list of names will eventually be compiled and sent to a person in a position of political power as a show of force, to try to make them care. It was a cause that I believed in strongly, back in those now-forgotten days when I used to believe in causes, and in chain emails too. So I signed my name at the bottom and sent it on to all my friends who were likely to feel the same way. I included Becky's e-mail address in the list.

The next day, she unexpectedly replied to my message. "Haven't seen you in a while," said her message. "How about a date? Becky."

That was the whole thing. I read it several times, which didn't take long, and found that I was sexually aroused just by Rebecca's use of the word, "date."

I called her on the phone, and we arranged to have lunch the next day. Sarah was out of town on a business trip, and she had the car, so Becky agreed to come by my apartment and pick me up.

I was all nervous as I waited for her. I tried to keep myself occupied, to distract myself from the tension of expectation, but I wasn't very good at it. Finally she knocked on the door. I ran over and opened it up.

"Hi, Brandon," she said.

"Hi, Becky, it's great to see you. Do you want to come in for a minute?"

She came in, I closed the door behind her and gave her a big hug. Neither of us seemed inclined to break the embrace, so we stood there holding each other until she pulled back just far enough to look me in the eyes. We smiled at each other then, in silent mutual understanding. I moved my face towards hers, and she simultaneously moved in towards me. Our kiss was long, protracted, perfect, magical. When at last we broke it off, I picked her up. She gave a small shriek but allowed me to carry her into the bedroom. I half-dropped her on the bed, a little ungracefully, and half-fell right on top of her. We continued kissing as we removed our shoes, then began unbuttoning and removing each other's clothes. When we were undressed, I rolled on top of her, erect and ready, kissing her mouth, holding one of her perfect breasts in my hand. She opened her legs to let me in between them. I got into position but before beginning I had brief second thoughts. *If she's got an STD,* I thought, *then I've probably already caught it from her, but...*

"Are you on the pill?" I asked.

She smiled, nodded, and pulled me towards her. I kissed her. Her lips parted, my tongue explored her wet mouth, and as we kissed, I entered her.

The sensation was as blindingly transcendent as it had been the first time, that night months ago when I'd fucked her from behind while she licked Nicky's pussy. This time it wasn't kinky, it was just the two of us, expressing love to each other with our bodies, making love, creating love, loving each other and feeling each other perfect in our fit. We moved together, we moaned together, we built up speed and got rowdy together. When she came, I knew it, and shortly afterwards, I felt a shock of pleasure so great it was almost painful as I released myself inside her.

We had renewed our bond, and this time, there was no going back to just being friends. We had created the kind of magic together that warps the fabric of the space-time continuum. Reality had changed while we made love, and it would never again go back to quite the same shape it had held before.

My juices mingled with Becky's juices, and dripped out onto the bed I shared with Sarah.

Becky and I took a quick shower together, and had lunch, laughing and talking, feeling that we were the best of friends, more than friends, the most beautifully perfect couple in all the world.

*   *   *

I felt this genuine deep romantic connection to Becky that I couldn't explain, couldn't get over, and I discovered that I really badly wanted to learn more about it, explore it, touch and feel and taste it until I had penetrated Becky's soul and pumped her as full of my life as I had pumped her full of drippy jizz that one night when she had joined me and Nicole for tequila and love.

And yet, somewhere in the back of my mind, I was still completely depressed about Nicky and ready to bang my head against the wall. I was pretty confused. I think the feelings alternated, some on some days, some on other days, happy to be back together with Sarah the love of my life, stoked to flirt with cute little sexy Becky, totally busted up that Nicole hated me so much. I'm fucking nuts, I tell you. Nuts, or just plain stupid.

*   *   *

And as I've already begun telling, that's when my real affair with Becky started, and in a way it was much worse than my affair with Nicole, I guess for a number of reasons. I hooked up with Nicole for a while at a time when I was having what felt like severe problems with my true primary relationship, and though I grew truly attached to her over time, for most of the time we were hanging out I mostly just thought of her as some girl I was sleeping with, and assumed that she similarly thought of me as just some guy in between her other boyfriends. That is bad, arguably, because maybe we weren't sufficiently respecting each other, but we both seemed to be comfortable with it, at first, so being casual wasn't too much of a problem until later.

But with Becky it was different. The wounds in my relationship with Sarah were on the mend, I had no reason to run away from it. Worse, I never thought of Becky as just some girl I was seeing. From the first time I met her I knew she was someone who I could really fall in love with; and after that first time we made love, even if it was in kind of a kinky situation that also involved a third person, I felt like we really had established a loving relationship with each other, I mean, at least every time we saw each other after that we would look into each other's eyes and smile in a certain way that seemed to recall that night and exchange smiles and looks that seemed to mean something to both of us; and although we hadn't acted on it again for a really long time, until after Sarah and I seemed to have solved all our problems and recommitted to each other, until after Nicky had the abortion and stopped speaking to me, until after Becky had broken up with Randy who I guess I didn't know about yet, until after Randy and Nicky had hooked up in a way that I would have wanted to be positive for Nicole but which was apparently so traumatic that it caused her to vent at me horribly in public: it was only *after* all that had happened that Becky and I started seeing each other regularly, and it was really bad timing.

*   *   *

I don't know, I was in a real strange frame of mind at the time. I think I was kind of crazy, or *really* crazy; but at the time it all seemed perfectly logical. I didn't feel like I was being psychopathic or pathological or whatever you want to call it; I felt like I was following my heart, the way they always tell you to do in children's books and inspirational speeches.

One night when I was sure that Nicole was working, I told Sarah that I was going in to the restaurant, which I did, but only for like ten minutes, to talk a little shop with Josh, the other night manager, and then I drove to Becky's apartment building.

I knew the code, so I let myself in at the outside door, climbed the stairs, and knocked at the door of apartment 212. After a few minutes, Becky opened it. She was wearing sweat-pants and a baggy, oversized T-shirt. She looked rumpled, maybe a little sleepy, and transcendentally, earth-shatteringly sexy.

"Nicole's out," she said when she saw me. "I think she's at work."

"I know," I said. She looked at me, maybe hoping I wouldn't say it. I said it. "I came to see you."

Becky shook her head. "I don't know if that's such a good idea, Brandon."

I should have been prepared for that, I suppose, but after the interactions I had been having with Becky recently I had thought she would be eager to engage in a private encounter with me. Apparently she was having second thoughts, and it took me a while to finally begin to stutter out, "Becky, I want you to understand."

"I think I understand perfectly," she said, raising one eyebrow at me.

"But there's more to it than just..." I let that one hang.

"What else could there be?" she asked suspiciously.

I looked around at the dingy apartment building hallway, and back at Becky standing in her open doorway. "Do I have to tell you from out here?"

"Oh, for God's sake," she said, and rolled her eyes. "All right, come in."

There were blankets on the couch, and a glass of wine on the living room table; as I was entering the room, the VCR came off pause. Becky impatiently stamped over to the remote control and turned off the TV. "I was watching a movie," she told me.

"I'm sorry to interrupt," I said, not least of all because it sounded as if maybe she'd rather be watching the movie than talking to me.

"It's all right," she said in that blunt tone and slightly drawling, nasal accent with which we Americans speak.

I stood by the couch, assuming she would return to her blanket nest there. Instead she asked, "Would you like something to drink?"

I hesitated, but finally I decided maybe it would help my nerves to be able to drink something. "Sure," I said. My voice wavered a little, and I cleared my throat and coughed a bit, maybe because I needed to, or maybe to cover up for my attack of nerves.

"What would you like?" she called from the kitchen, where I could hear the sound of cupboards and glasses.

"I don't know," I replied truthfully. Alcohol sounded both appealing and unnecessary; I wanted this to go smoothly. I didn't want my head to be any fuzzier than it already was. "What are you having?" I asked.

"I was thinking about some tea," she said.

"What?" I asked, because her voice was a bit muffled.

"Tea!" she called more loudly. "I'm having tea!"

I decided I didn't want us to keep shouting back and forth, so I followed her into the kitchen.

"Tea sounds good," I said. She must not have heard me walk in because she totally jumped.

"Jesus," she said, "you scared the shit out of me."

"Sorry, I thought you heard me come in."

"It's OK. What kind of tea do you like?"

"Do you have green tea?"

"Organic, with puffed brown rice," she said. God, she was so my kind of woman. I wanted her so badly, I desired to possess her and to love her, for the simple reason that she didn't seem to have any major flaws.

So obviously I had green tea. She had chamomile. I stood behind her as she put the water on the stove to boil. We weren't really talking, each lost in thought, I guess. I watched her small frame, for she was kind of short, but so nicely built, with all the right curves, her ass outlined against her sweat pants, the roundness of her breasts which even the baggiest of T-shirts could never conceal, her waist, so nicely curved that as I looked, I wanted to put my hands there. In fact I allowed this urge to seize control of my mind, the logical arguments against such an action seemed so inconsequential that I did it. I just stepped close to her and wrapped my arms around her waist. I put my hands on the curve at the bottom of her belly, just below her belly button. I pressed my face into her hair, I pressed my body against hers. I could feel the tension of my erection against the small of her back and I'm sure she could feel it too. We stood like that, for a moment, and she started to cover my hands with hers, but then she suddenly pushed them away, instead, and stepped away from me.

"Brandon," she said, "you're already engaged to somebody, plus you've been sleeping with my roommate. I've been thinking about it a lot, and I really don't see how you and I could possibly have any kind of healthy relationship."

"But the other night-" I began, in reference to the last time I'd seen her. That night, we had rather enthusiastically given in to temptation and gotten down and dirty.

"It was a mistake, Brandon, a bad idea," said Becky, shaking her lovely head. "We never should have gone there."

"I didn't think it was a mistake at all," I argued. I felt like arguing. I felt like she wanted me to feel ashamed and humbled, and that irked me. I hoped I didn't sound like a goddamn sniveling whiner as I tried to explain my state of mind. "We did it on purpose, and it was really good," I reminded her. "It wasn't a mistake," I insisted. "We had built up to that incident over a long period of time; and you know it, Becky."

She tried to interrupt me, before I could get started on one of my tirades; but I wouldn't let her: instead, I kept talking fast so she wouldn't have any space to cut in.

"You and I have *more* than just a lot in common," I gushed romantically. "We connect with each other in a really unusual and unbelievably good way. I feel really close to you."

I couldn't quite tell from the way she was looking at me what she was thinking, so I blundered on with my little speech, and she turned her back again as I continued.

"Every time I see you," I spilled my guts to her, "I feel like I could just plug my head into yours and relax in bliss for a while, just sharing our understanding of each other and how happy we are to be together. I want to be with you, Becky, because you and I work so well together. I want you to be a part of my life."

Beautiful Becky turned to face me once again. Now that I had run out of words, I looked her deeply in the eyes. She looked back at me, totally expressionless. She was so expressionless that she looked almost angry; but she returned my gaze, so I figured that was a good sign. Neither of us said anything for a while. Then she turned away again and gazed out the window. The water began to boil. Neither of us moved.

"You don't even know me," she said eventually, and turned to the stove.

My strong hands upon her trembling shoulders, I gently turned her around until she was looking into my eyes once more. I could feel that electrical surge when our eyes made contact, and I knew she could feel it, too. "I know everything I need, to know that I am looking forward to learning more about you."

She looked away, frowned, shook her head, and removed herself from my grip a second time. "I'm not sure it's what I want, Brandon."

"That could be a problem," I admitted.

At this, she looked longingly into my eyes, for a moment; then looked away wordlessly.

I waited until she had poured the hot water and put down the kettle; then for the third time that evening, I took hold of her body. I turned her around again, and looked her in the eyes again, and I was pleased to note that her eyes were watering: not pleased because I wanted her to be sad; but rather, pleased because, if she was sad then maybe it was a validation of what I had been saying. Maybe it meant that she felt something for me after all. I had begun to worry. But as long as she had feelings for me, then everything would be okay.

I embraced her, and this time her hands returned the pressure on my back. We stood there like that, I don't know, it seemed like a long time, just holding each other, neither of us wanting to move, because when one of us moved, time would start again and we would have to make a decision and we both feared that decision.

I wish I could just end the story right there, with my arms around Rebecca and her arms around me, as hope and fear diminished into insignificance next to the unsurpassable feeling that in that one moment, all that mattered was that we were there together. But we were unable to freeze time forever. She shifted a little bit, and I started letting my hands roam across her back, down to her firm little round buttocks. She squirmed and pulled back, not breaking contact completely, but just lightly resting her fingertips on my waist.

"Do you understand?" I asked. The question was ambiguous. The unspoken implications were meant to ask, *Do you understand how I feel about you? Do you understand that this relationship has a greater chance than most to be truly sparkly and amazing? Do you understand that of all the women I love, I love you the most? Do you understand that I love you so much it hurts, so much that I want to just throw everything else away and give myself to you completely?*

She didn't answer that. Instead she said, "How do I know that in another four months you won't be spouting the same lines to some other chick, whoever happens to erect your fancy at the moment?" She gestured with a finger to emphasize her evocative choice of words.

"Becky, I don't think you understand. You could be The One just as easily as Sarah could. You're really-"

"But the thing is," she interrupted me, "that you are engaged to her. Weren't you sure, when you got engaged to her, that she was the only one you'd ever want to be with, ever again?"

"Well, yes, but, no! I don't even know," I admitted, confused. "I didn't even really think about it. It just seemed appropriate, you know?"

"Right," said Becky, in a tone of voice that said I was full of shit. "And now?"

"Now, I don't see how I can only be with her for the rest of my life when I feel this way about you," I confessed wholeheartedly.

"What kind of a crap line is that?" she demanded.

"It's not a-"

"Brandon, I wish I felt like I could trust you."

"You can trust me!"

"But I can't. You've cheated on two women within the past how many weeks? It wouldn't be-"

"You can't say I cheated on Nicole!"

"Yes I can, because you did, with me."

"What you and I did had no effect on my relationship with Nicole."

"Did you ask her?"

"No I didn't ask her!" I said, louder than I'd meant to, "and I don't see why I should have to ask her, based on the fact that we totally broke up already, and now she's been sleeping with this guy Randy..."

"She what?" Becky asked, her face betraying a surprisingly vivid emotional response. We had moved back into the living room early in this exchange. I had sat down on the couch, hoping she would sit next to me, but instead she'd chosen a big chair across from me, tucking her feet up underneath her. The revelation about Randy seemed to have surprised and upset her far more than anything else about my visit.

"I would have thought that you knew," I said, slowly and quite truthfully.

"Nicole is with Randy?" Becky asked. "Are you sure?" She looked almost angry, her eyes wide. She nearly spilled her tea.

"Well, I mean, that's what she told me. Why? Do you know him?"

She nodded and turned her head away.

"Who is he?"

She didn't say anything for one of those periods of time that seems really long but probably wasn't. I sipped my tea & didn't say anything. It was excellent tea, aromatic, not bitter. I took out my teabag, placed it on a saucer that had already been sitting on the table. Finally she took a deep breath and, still looking away, she said, "Randy is my boyfriend. *Was* my boyfriend. We got in a fight and sort of broke up a week, maybe a week and a half ago."

I let that process for a few seconds. "I see," I said eventually. "I guess I didn't know that you'd had a boyfriend this whole time." She looked away; the omission had clearly been deliberate. "And you didn't know, uh, Nicole didn't mention to you, that she'd been... Well, I'm sorry. Really. I hate to be the bearer of bad news."

She turned her face back towards me. She really was crying now, but she gave me a pathetic little smile through her tears. "It's all right, it's not your fault. I'm sorry I'm reacting like this. I suppose I should have known something like this was coming, I just didn't expect it quite so soon."

I wasn't sure if I should encourage her to tell me or try to change the subject. As I hesitated, she continued.

"We had been together for two and a half years," Becky explained.

"I'm sorry," I said again. I didn't really know what else to say. I considered the implications: how circumstances like this would statistically tend to predict a discouraging forecast regarding the consequences of any attempt at a romantic entanglement between Becky and myself; and also, if they had only broken up a week and a half ago, then she had already previously cheated on Randy with me, twice. What a twisted mess.

She hadn't said anything else, and I still didn't know what to say, so I stupidly repeated myself, and said again, "Sorry to bring you bad news."

"It's all right," she reiterated. Then at last Becky looked me in the eye and opened up to me. "He was an asshole," she told me bluntly. "We weren't suited for each other." She smiled again, then shook her head and looked away. "But he was an asshole that I loved. I mean, two and a half years..."

"That's a big chunk of your life," I agreed empathetically, thinking to myself that Sarah and I had been together even longer. We had actually been living together for two and a half years. And how long had we been together before we moved in together?

"Yeah," Becky said, clearly still thinking about that big chunk of her life.

"I've been engaged to Sarah for about that long," I told her.

"Randy and I never made that kind of commitment," Becky sighed. "But it was for the best. I'm just... still getting used to it. I'm okay." She looked at her mug of tea as if she'd forgotten it was there, took a sip, and put it down on the table. Then she changed the subject.

"So," she said, "have you told Sarah about Nicole and me yet?"

"Uh," I said, "well, to tell you the truth, no, honestly, I haven't, uh, thought of a good way to break it to her."

"Over a nice romantic dinner at a fancy restaurant?" Becky suggested.

I frowned. "No, I can't really say that sounds like such a good idea to me."

"That's where Randy and I broke up."

"Seems like a bad place for an argument."

"Oh, it was."

I told her my similar story. "Nicole chewed me out in the middle of a crowded kitchen at the restaurant, once. It was really embarrassing."

"Yeah," Becky said, but then relentlessly persisted in being my conscience. "But really, Brandon, don't you think Sarah would want to know to the truth?"

"Well, yeah, but, I don't know what to tell her."

"Just tell her what you did. It's better if she finds out from you, in person."

"I can't see how anything at all would be 'better' in this situation."

"Don't be stubborn."

"Okay," I said, stubbornly. "But what about you?"

"What about me?"

"Do I get to know you better or not?"

"Are you, or are you not, sitting with me in my living room, having a very personal conversation with me? If this isn't getting to know me better, then what is it that you're looking for?"

"Oh, this is wonderful," I hastened to assure her. "And I want to spend lots of time doing this, talking with you like this." *But I also want to spend lots of time having lots of hot sex with you, too,* I thought, but I didn't say it. It turned out to be okay that I didn't say it, though, because based on what she did next, she must have been thinking the same thing.

Becky put down her tea, stepped over to the couch, and sat on my lap facing me. I kissed her and lay back. She began grinding against me, dry humping me as I felt her up, and we kissed some more. I suppose anybody can imagine where this led, and I've already filled this manuscript with sex scenes. Suffice to say that the love Becky and I made together was incredible, some of the best in my life, without any practice together, without hardly moving, there was just something about our respective shapes, sizes, and textures that fit in a way that felt nothing short of perfect. More importantly, when we had sex, we weren't just fucking, we really were making love: it felt like an expression of a deep connection between two people who knew each other far better than we could easily explain.

*   *   *

I left Becky's place that night feeling wonderful. I was supercharged with happiness and love: love for myself (a welcome change from my habitual self-loathing); love for three women who I knew intimately; and love for the world in general. That's pretty good, for me; usually the best I can muster is a bleak acceptance of the world in general: so if I'm actually feeling love for the world, then you know I'm having a pretty fucking amazingly good day.

As I drove from my newest lover's place back to the apartment I shared with my fiancée, I thought about the two of them. I really felt like I loved both Sarah and Becky. My relationship with Becky was fresh and new and therefore exciting and stimulating, but my relationship with Sarah was warm and dependable, and the love I felt for her ran deep, despite the other feelings which had unfortunately been introduced into our relationship and hadn't quite been resolved yet. For, even though on the surface Sarah and I had begun to sort out our differences, on a deeper level the unspoken rift which we had allowed to grow between us had allowed a chill breeze to blow into our warm happy life together; and I, instead of trying to fix it, had run to the arms of other lovers; and Sarah, maybe she wasn't sure it was worth fixing, so she didn't really do anything about it either, for a long time: until eventually, at some point she began to make an effort, she tried asking me out on dates and stuff, although by then I had caused damage that she didn't yet know about, which would eventually end up...

Anyway enough of me blabbing.

When I got home that night, I found that Sarah had gone on a cleaning frenzy while I was away. She'd tidied up the whole apartment, and lit candles all around the place. When I came in, she was listening to some downtempo jazz music and reading a book, with a glass of wine next to her. She got up and came over to kiss me. She was wearing her sexiest nightgown, with her hair pulled loosely back, and as she stood close, saying hello, I could smell alcohol on her breath; this wasn't her first glass of wine.

"How was work?" she asked innocently.

"Oh, it was fine," I lied, suddenly feeling terrible that I had so brazenly gone over to Becky's house for most of the evening and left my beautiful Sarah alone.

"I've been waiting for you," she whispered, and kissed me so sweetly, her moist lips tenderly pulling on mine. I put my hands on her back and felt the firmness of her shapely body through the silken fabric of her gown, and she held me close, and once again I wish I could end the story right there, while everything was still wonderful and all the world full of love and bliss.

But events didn't stop for my whims. Time continued to move, and though I don't believe in fate as predetermined destiny, one might say that I had already created my own fate, and was drawn inexorably on towards it.

It didn't seem like a bad thing at the time. Sarah and I made love right there, on the living room couch (my second couch of the evening, in fact); and it felt very different from how it had felt with Becky: but all the same, there was a certain similarity to the experience... Then, oh my love, Sarah and I were not just fucking, we were making love, oh yes, we were telling each other things with our bodies, things we already knew but loved to be told over and over and over. We touched and rubbed each other, moved hands and fingers over skin and hair, pushed and ground hips, and kissed each other's faces, necks, shoulders, elsewhere...

I was above Sarah, rocking on my knees, and her lips, below me, were brushing my neck and shoulders, back and forth, now and then opening slightly in a kiss. Suddenly she stopped moving with me, and though I kept going, I was required to change the rhythm of my movement somewhat, and looked down to see what Sarah was experiencing. She was looking intently at a spot on my shoulder, right at the base of my neck. She glanced up into my eyes, then back down at this spot; then she put her fingers there, closed her eyes, and kissed my cheek. A moment later I found that she was pushing me away, up and off her, and I pulled back and rolled off the couch, and I thought the trouble was going to start then, but she turned over and rose up on her knees, caught my arm and pulled me back over to her, shoved me down on my back and positioned herself above me. Her eyes closed, she reached down, took me in her hand and placed me there, then sat back against me hard, her eyebrows up, her mouth open, her eyes closed. She kept her eyes closed, her face pointed towards the ceiling, as she moved up and down on me, riding my cock, and soon she was going fast, pushing hard, slamming herself against me, biting her lip as she worked, she was getting rough with me, I felt a little sore already but didn't mind. A shudder began to work its way down her back, and she moaned, her face creased in an expression as of extreme anguish; then working herself back and forth in a violent frenzy until she shook with spasms, she cried out, then folded herself down on me and lay still. She pressed her cheek against mine and I could feel that it was wet with tears.

"Sarah," I said, "I love you."

She nodded, not saying anything, her nose pressed into my neck. Then, aware that I hadn't come when she did, she wordlessly rearranged our bodies again into my favorite position and moved with me, accepting me, squeezing me, taking me in, welcoming my climax and the accompanying burst of liquid warmth.

I hugged her tight from behind, squeezed her and kissed her face as romantically as I could from this angle. "Sarah," I said again, just to hear the sound of her name.

Sarah kissed my cheek, a quick peck, then shook her head "no." She still had her eyes closed, and she shook her head like that, back and forth, disconsolate, until she burst out crying.

"Oh Sarah Sarah," I said; but it didn't help that I was thinking of her now, it was already too late by then.

She rolled over to face me and we put our arms around each other but she still didn't look at me. "Brandon," she said, "you've meant everything to me for so long, I can't imagine life without you."

"I don't want you to imagine that," I said. "I want us to be together."

"But what are we doing wrong, Brandon?" she said. "Why does it feel so bad?"

"Oh baby," I said, "I think it's already getting to be so much better. We had a little negative energy between us for a while, but it's improving, right now it feels so good to be with you, and what we just did, that was really amazing."

She didn't answer for a while, didn't look at me, just lay naked on the couch as love juices leaked out and down the inside of her thigh.

"I feel like I'm losing you," she said finally.

"But I'm right here."

"We never talk anymore."

"We're talking now," I protested. "And we had a great talk the other night, too, remember that?"

"I feel like you don't really let me in."

"Sometimes I feel that way, from you, too," I said.

"But Brandon," she said, "I never shut you out!"

"And yet," I explained quietly, "there are times when I sometimes feel totally cut off from you."

She lay quiet a moment, summoning the power to spring with her next weapon. "Maybe we'll always be cut off," she said finally. "Maybe we'll never really connect again."

"What are you talking about, Sarah?" I said. I was starting to get worried. "I feel like I'm connecting with you right now."

"But now it's so *complicated!*" she cried out, another tear appearing at the corner of her eye and describing a delicate arc down her cheek. "It used to be so simple, just you and me and our love, and the rest of the world could just kiss off; but now, Brandon, I don't know if we'll ever be able to *trust* each other again."

"Sarah," I said, "in all the ways that really count, I will always trust you, and I hope you will always know that I am always there for you, I want you to feel like you can trust me, I want you to feel like I-"

"But I can't, Brandon, I can't."

"Sarah, Sarah, what are you talking about?"

She wouldn't answer me, just pulled away from me and cried, lying there naked on the couch. I decided I could probably guess why she was upset. She had figured it out somehow. I went in to the bathroom and took a leak. I looked in the mirror. My face appeared haggard and stressed out, pale, unshaven, blotchy, prematurely wrinkled, with a nasty pimple erupting on the side of my nose and dark shadowy rings under my eyes. My appearance now was like a different person from how I had felt just an hour before. I looked closer. To my horror, I saw a small purple bruise on my shoulder, right there at the base of my neck. It was only minor, superficial, unintentional, but it was very clearly a hickey, and clearly it had not been made by Sarah, whose height naturally placed her mouth higher up on my neck.

She knew. I was totally fucked.

I went back out to the couch. Sarah hadn't moved. I sat down next to her and took her hand in mine. She didn't react or say anything.

"I'll never feel differently about you," I told Sarah.

"I used to think that everything could be perfect forever," she answered eventually.

"I don't see why we should have to change anything," I said. We were having this disjointed conversation, each making remarks that only tangentially related to the other's words, until she spoke again.

"Everything has changed already," she told me.

"But Sarah," I argued desperately, "I love you so much and I always will. I don't ever want to let you go."

"And I will always love you, Brandon," she told the cushion nearest her face, "but at the same time I feel you slipping away. My dream is dying – my dream of *us*, I'm afraid it can never be."

"I'm not going anywhere," I said, "I'm right here. Keep the dream alive."

"Brandon," she said, "I'm scared. I don't know what's true or real anymore. I don't know what I want, I don't know what I feel, I don't know what I'm supposed to do about all the things that I know. I used to think... I used to think so many things. I used to think it was forever."

"It is forever!" I almost shouted.

"Maybe forever in a different way," she said, "but never the same again. Never the same."

"Sarah!" I called her, and we argued and cried for hours; but although she stayed with me for another month or two, she was already gone, far beyond the point where I could get her back, and it was completely my own stupid fault because I had pushed her away with infidelity and lies.

*   *   *

Actually, after her initial reaction, Sarah seemed pretty calm about the whole thing. She asked me some questions, and I finally tried to be honest with her, belatedly, and she was hurt, and told me so quite frankly. When I reminded her that I would always love her, well looking back I suppose she could have said something like, "what kind of shit is that?" but she didn't, she agreed with me, that our hearts would remain linked indefinitely.

What we did was, we agreed to try having an open relationship. I swore to Sarah that my love for her was so strong that no matter what I did or how I felt about other people, it could never make me love her any less. I meant that. It was true. It is still true.

Sarah expressed reservations, understandably. But after a moment's thought, she declared her feeling of trust for me to be so completely shattered that she didn't want to enter back into our previous understanding of monogamy; because, she explained quite reasonably, she would be perpetually concerned that I would go behind her back again, and that she'd rather have it out in the open. I assumed that she had a secondary motive – that she wanted our relationship to be open so she too could get it on with someone else, whether for revenge, or freedom, or just to spread the love around, the reason was unimportant, I felt that she had a right to, and on some level I think I hoped that this would somehow expiate my own sins

For a time it almost seemed like it was going to work. Sarah and I felt close to each other in a new kind of honesty we'd never shared before, the honesty of doubts, fears, illusions and previously unmentionable infidelities of the mind and body.

Yes, as it turned out, Sarah had spent some time with another man while I was out with Nicole once or twice, and I hadn't known about it. She didn't really answer me when I asked whether or not she had sex with him, so once again I have to assume that she did, or at least sucked him off, although, maybe that's just the story I tell myself so I won't feel so guilty; but my point is, as I said before, it really doesn't matter, it couldn't make me love her less. Nothing could make me love her less, not even jealousy. I was living in the fantasy that she felt the same way about me. I told her about Nicole and Becky; just in general terms, not graphic details that would stick in her mind. I was so gullible, I was really prepared to believe that our love could last like that.

I even went out with Becky, a couple times, during that period. I told her that I had come clean with Sarah. I didn't tell her about the monstrous irony of the situation: that on the night when Becky had told me that I should come clean to Sarah, she herself left the mark which spoke for itself. Becky seemed relieved that everything was finally out in the open; and for a while, at least, both she and Sarah seemed more or less content with the situation. I had some initial misgivings of my own, which eventually turned out to be well-founded; but at first nothing bad seemed to be happening, so I tried to ignore my second-guesses and be content in the knowledge that I loved and was loved by two very beautiful women.

I feel like I should say more about that period of time, though I don't know what, exactly. It lasted for a while, almost two months, I guess, and Sarah was once again my primary lover and I was once again swearing undying love to her; but after that one night, we never discussed fidelity again, although it became understood, or at least I thought it was, that we loved each other regardless of whether or not we restricted our sexual encounters to just each other. I didn't tell her, exactly, when I went out with Becky, but I never lied, either, and I'm pretty sure she knew, though she didn't say anything about it to me. Similarly, she went out a few times, and I don't know where she went or who she went with, and I didn't ask, but she came home to me afterward, and I figured that was what mattered.

I'm trying to remember if I ever really thought it would work, stupid, stupid me. Probably I didn't give the matter much thought; and the *reason* for that is that I never thought anything could really come between us, even when we were facing each other from receding banks on the opposite sides of a widening chasm; I thought we would always come back to each other because of the strength of the bond that held us together.

So yes, I did think the arrangement would work, without questioning. I simply believed, deep down in my soul, that Sarah and I were inseparable in the long run.

*   *   *

In fact, to be perfectly honest, I liked it. After a while I got over my Nicole-related mood swings, and actually managed to feel pretty groovy. I felt wide awake and alive, I was in a good mood all the time, I felt love for everything and every measly moron that I saw, I had a very laid-back and philosophical attitude towards all problems that came my way. Sarah and I had worked past our petty grudges and started hanging out together again. We found time to go out to dinner together, to go see movies together, to have a lot of really great sex together. And that was awesome.

And it was only better because when a couple days did happen to go by when Sarah's and my moods or schedules failed to intersect, every so often I would hang out with Becky. Nicole had moved out to live with Randy, and Becky had found another roommate, so on those evenings when it seemed appropriate, I could just go over to her place and we would drink some wine and eat some pasta and have some really great sex, incredible, mind-blowing, picture-perfect sex, the exquisite sex of fantasies and your favorite masturbation memories.

Whenever I saw Becky, I had a great time, I felt increasingly happy to share time with her. She was crazy and sarcastic and fun, and we had really great sex together. Had I mentioned that yet? The more we hung out together, though, the more we discovered that we really did have a lot in common, beyond just the mutual physical attraction; and that our personalities and temperaments were ideally suited for each other. When we hung out, we engaged each other intellectually, gave value to each other's ideas, filled each other with humor and happiness and insights into life and love and the nature of being. Being together was always joyful.

I will always be glad that I got to know her in that way, though it made the later betrayal that much more painful.

But mostly, it seemed to me that Sarah was my primary focus at that time. I was having such a great time with Sarah that she and I talked about all our plans for the future, got really excited about our discussions of houses and gardens and children. She was beautiful and sweet and honest, or at least I thought so, maybe she wasn't really telling me everything. I felt really close to her, though, and I thought she felt really close to me. It seemed as if we had brought our relationship to a new stage, more exciting than ever before.

Neither of them seemed to mind the arrangement, as far as I could tell. For probably about two months or more, the situation seemed to be going really well. I got along with both of my lovers; and really as far as I could tell, they both got along with me. Both appeared to enjoy my company, told me at times that they thought highly of me in many ways, in bed and out of it; both even spoke of their emotional attachments to me. Nobody was voicing any dissatisfaction anywhere. As far as I knew, we were all having a great time.

I didn't want this situation to change; but nothing is static, and a balance as fragile as the one I just described cannot be sustained for long. Sooner or later somebody or other will end up feeling slighted, and then it all ends badly.

* * *

Sarah had been out for most of the afternoon. I'd been home alone, drinking some beers, working on a little side project and taking it easy. After she'd been gone for several hours, I began to wonder what Sarah was doing; but I figured it was her freedom, her prerogative, her right to do whatever she wanted. Nonetheless I felt flooded with relief when I heard her come home. I tramped up the stairs from the basement of the compact little duplex we shared, and met her in the living room.

"Hi, honey," I said, "how are you?"

"Fine," she said tersely, and allowed me to give her a quick hug, then pulled away, ostensibly to put her coat in the closet.

I stepped in behind her and put my arms around her with my hands on her belly. "I've been thinking about you all day," I told her. "Did you have a good time?"

"Mmm hmm," was the only answer I got out of her. Then she broke away and started to walk off.

"Hey," I said.

"Hey, what?" she asked, impatiently.

"Come here." I tried to hold her close. Once again she pulled away after I had given her just a brief hug.

"Have to go to the bathroom," she mumbled, extracting herself from my arms and walking down the hall. I sat down on the couch and waited for her to come back out. When she did, she walked right past me, into the kitchen, avoiding my gaze. I knew, then, with absolute certainty, that she'd been with another lover, but I still felt convinced that I didn't need to be bothered by that, that there was no reason for such a thing to come between the two of us, and I wanted to try to show Sarah that it was okay, that I didn't mind, that everybody could love everybody else and it didn't need to create harsh feelings.

I followed Sarah into the kitchen. She was making herself some tea.

"Have you eaten dinner yet?" I asked.

"Not hungry," she replied. She still didn't look at me.

"Oh, but hey," I said, trying to be jocular, attempting to lift up the sullen mood she was exuding, "you have to watch your nutrition!"

"Don't criticize me," she said sharply.

"Hey, now," I said, trying to remain calm, "I'm just trying to make a joke, there's no need to get all bent out of shape."

"I would appreciate it if you limited your humor to things that don't concern my personal habits," she told me sternly, stirring some honey into her beverage. "I get tired of your criticism."

"Sarah, honey, I wasn't trying to criticize you, I can't remember the last time I was inclined to criticize you. You're fine, relax, don't worry, you're perfect, I love you for who you are, that's all there is." Finally she allowed me to rest one arm around her waist. I took the opportunity to draw her near and plant a kiss on her cheek. She stonily ignored it, taking a sip of her tea.

Bloody great conversationalist you are today, I thought, but didn't say that. Instead I tried to fill the silence with lighthearted chatter about my side project, which was just some typical guy thing, it doesn't even matter if it was carpentry or auto maintenance or soldering a custom circuitboard. Lighthearted chatter doesn't necessarily come naturally to me, I usually allow it to be supplied by whatever women are in the room, but I thought I was doing pretty well. Sarah seemed to be thawing a little bit, allowing me to stroke her back and buttocks as I talked and she sipped her tea. I found that I was becoming sexually aroused by my proximity to her, and as I thought about it, I realized that it had been a few days since my last sexual encounter. I thought to myself that now would be a good time to rectify the whole situation through some spine-tingling lovemaking with Sarah, the love of my life.

So right in the middle of some stupid sentence, I moved my face in close to Sarah's from where I was standing beside her, and I opened up my lips and started sucking on her earlobe; and at the same time, I grabbed myself a handful of her fine, tight ass.

"Brandon!" she reprimanded me as she stepped all the way across the room to get away from me, "can't you see I'm not in the mood?"

"But why not, baby, what's wrong?"

"I'm just not, so leave it alone."

"But what am I going to do about this?" I asked, indicating my erection, which was visibly outlined as a bulge in the front of my trousers. It was, perhaps, the worst thing I could have said in that moment.

"I don't care what you do," she snarled, "go bang it against a wall or something, just don't bother me with it."

"Sarah, what's the matter?"

"Brandon, I don't think you really want to know."

"No really I do, please tell me."

She didn't reply at first. I had to encourage her. Finally she said, "Well first of all, I've already had enough sex for one day, and I don't want any more."

Yes, that stung. It hurt real bad. Having her go out with another lover was one thing. Having her reject me because someone else had already satisfied her urges for the day, that was something else, a good deal more disturbing. I think I started to mumble out something along those lines; but by then she had started talking, and she wasn't done yet.

"You should have expected this," she told me coldly. "It's a direct consequence of your brilliant open relationship arrangement." I tried to remind her that it hadn't been entirely *just* my idea, but she didn't give me a chance. "What did you think was going to happen?" she demanded rhetorically. "Do you think I exist to just sit around and be fucked all the time? There's more to life than just sex, and I'm going to be really sore if I have any more today. I'm not always in the mood just because *you* want some."

"That might be a little more detail than I needed right there," I grumbled.

"Well at least I'm telling the truth!" she shouted at me.

"I don't fucking care if it's the truth!" I shouted back. We were both pissed off by now, raging furious.

I don't even remember what we said next, nothing productive I'm sure; no actual communication was possible at that moment, for our minds were both filled with the red hot glare of unreasoning fury, and if you've ever been overtaken by it, then you know that when you are in the grip of such a rage, logic and reality recede, your senses become dull and distant, your vision fades, all your awareness is temporarily suspended but for the all-encompassing fire of anger, passion, weakness, fury, fear, death, screaming anguish and hatred. One accesses a sub-level of the human consciousness which links directly to animal instinct and temporarily disables normal thought patterns. Sarah and I, the woman I loved more than anything in the world and the man she had once pledged her life to, we turned that rage against each other, and it was the worst thing I have ever felt. My beloved and I created hell on earth, right there in our kitchen, and as it blazed, we burned each other in its fires.

It makes me feel so sad, just to think about it, and angry, too, but mostly just sad, now; and I can't escape the knowledge that really it was all my fault.

Well, eventually Sarah came out with what was really on her mind.

"I'm not satisfied with this relationship," Sarah told me. "I feel like the trust between us has been violated and neither of us is sufficiently committed to put the work into the thing and fix it."

"But we've been working-" I began.

"It's just been getting worse!" she said angrily, "and it's only going to keep getting worse. You and I are just hurting each other now, and I don't think it's healthy for us to continue to try to be together."

"Sarah," I protested, "I haven't felt at all that all we're doing is hurting-"

"All the going around!" she cried out. "It's really getting to me! All I want is to be loved by one person, just one! One person who only loves one person, me! I don't want to have a fucking string of lovers! I don't want my goddamned boyfriend to have a fucking string of girlfriends, either! It makes me feel like just a face in the crowd, it doesn't make me happy, it makes me feel so bad."

"Sarah, why didn't you say this before?"

"I did say this before, and you weren't listening!"

"You didn't say it like *that*."

"Maybe I didn't understand it that way, before; but I do now, so I'm saying it."

"Well," I said hesitantly, "do you want to go back to..."

But she knew what I was going to say, and she cut me off before I had a chance to say it. "It's too late, Brandon," she said. "It's not fun with you any more. This is not working for me. It hasn't been working for a long time. You liked it like that. I didn't, but I don't want to change you, I want to find somebody who's happy with just *me*, and Scott's been asking me for quite a while now..."

*   *   *

That night, I went out and got real drunk at a bar, sitting by myself, the stereotypical depressed jilted loner loser. I think I tried to call Becky but got her answering machine; I think I left a really long, really stupid, drunken voice message, or maybe even two messages, no doubt telling her all sorts of things she didn't want to hear from me. I went home and Sarah was asleep in bed. I looked in at her as she lay in bed, so lovely, so peaceful, her face relaxed as she wandered through Dreamland. I swayed, put my hand on the door frame to steady myself. Went into the kitchen, got the last beer out of the fridge, chugged it, belched. Maybe found some whiskey or something in a cupboard. Maybe smoked some grass. I hardly remember but it seems likely. Generally abused myself. Got real dizzy. Went into the bathroom and puked it all up.

Sarah came in to wipe my face. Told her to go away, said I didn't want her to see me like this. "Poor Brandon," she cooed gently. She gave me a hug and I let her hold me. "Poor baby," she said, rocking me back and forth. Why had she waited for me to humiliate myself before she expressed these tender feelings? Her tenderness was pity; not respect.

I woke up on the bathroom floor, lying on my side in the position they teach you about when you take basic First Aid and they tell you the position that an unconscious or very drunk person should be placed in so they won't choke on their own vomit or their tongue or something. Daylight was coming in through the window. I felt like shit. My mouth tasted terrible. The room smelled like puke. My shirt was all splattered and stained. I tried to get myself cleaned up a bit, then went out into the house.

Sarah wasn't there. Neither was her suitcase, or her favorite clothes, or her toothbrush, or her birth-control pills.

I haven't seen her much since. She came back a few weeks later for the rest of her stuff, but I was at work. She helped me out with the rent, at first, since she had co-signed the lease and everything, but the lease is up soon, and now I'm going to have to move. Maybe that's okay, everything about this place reminds me of her, all the time. We've talked a couple times, and she was civil, almost friendly, but it hurt so much, so very very much... These days, even though it kills me to go without hearing her voice, I never try to contact her, because seeing her and knowing that I lost her is so much worse.

*　　*　　*

Well, I was pretty depressed about that, because despite the way it sounds from the coldly written statement of all the shitty things I did, I really loved Sarah more than anyone or anything else, and when she left me, well that hurt real bad, and I allowed myself to wallow in self-pity, I fell into a deep pit of depression, and if you've ever experienced one of *those*, then you know that while you are under its influence, your reasoning ability completely abandons you; your mind and all your senses are shut down; it's like everywhere you go, there's a really thick fog, even indoors, and everything sounds like there's cotton in your ears, and your skin is all numb, and you don't really notice what you're eating or what you're doing or where you're going or what people are saying to you, and afterwards your memory of the entire time period is hazy and patchy, not much sticks because nothing you're experiencing is at all related to where your body happens to be. Even if your mouth is moving and you're compelled to interact with people, you hardly notice, because the whole time, you're filled with a sinking feeling like you're drowning, and you've lost all hope of ever being rescued.

*   *   *

Although I was really brokenhearted about my loss of Sarah, at the same time I felt increasingly passionate about Becky, and I went out of my way to let her know how special she was to me. I took her out, cooked for her at home, wrote her little notes & left them where she would find them, bought her some sexy underwear, performed sexual favors without being asked, hell I even bought her flowers one time.

All the same, I was deeply unsettled about the breakup with Sarah. Becky mentioned several times, she was dubious about what this might mean for the eventual outcome of our relationship together. We tried, though, for a while, and I honestly put a lot of energy into trying to make it work.

Becky was, and is, a really amazing woman, so beautiful and so down to earth and so *real* that it was easy for me to love her; and once we were involved in a way that was just me and her, it was easy for me to tell her so.

Becky seemed to like it, at first, when I told her that I loved her; she even whispered the words back to me, smiling, snuggled up against me after we'd made the sweetest love ever.

In the course of several long discussions, Becky and I had come to the conclusion that our respective previous open relationships, hers with Randy and mine with Sarah, had not worked out as we had originally intended. Our open relationships with other people had left us both feeling hurt and under-appreciated; in fact, it was the supposed "openness" of my relationship with Sarah (for which I can claim credit, of course, there ain't nobody else to blame here), as well as the openness of Becky's relationship with Randy (which I know I haven't talked about much, basically he started that, but she wasn't really into it, kind of hoped that he'd get over it, but he never did; she only took advantage of the "open relationship" clause twice with me and maybe once with somebody else) – the openness of both relationships could be directly traced to their eventual demise. Becky and I got along so well that we decided we wanted to make it work between us, so we agreed to be completely monogamous with each other. Whatever her motivations may have been, I can't say, although I certainly thought I understood at the time. Personally, I felt like I had really fucked up with Sarah, with the lies and the cheating, and it had made me feel so bad; I thought since I liked Becky so much, that I could chase all the bad feelings away and replace them with good ones, and all we had to do was feel special and unique to each other.

It sounded great in theory. We both agreed to give it a shot. I was as stoked as a chronically depressed part-time alcoholic can be when he's just lost a fiancée. I mean, because like I said, I was really into her, and I went out of my way to make her feel special.

I can't believe I'm still writing this all out. I've been working on it for so long. I'm almost done. I'm going to sort of skip a lot of details because I have a deadline to keep, and I have to finish writing all this out so I can burn it and symbolically erase this whole part of my life in time to start a new one.

*   *   *

It was great at first. We spent a lot of time together, got on well, laughed a lot, stayed over at each other's places often, went out to movies & meals, had a great time together, and made a point of consciously enjoying our relationship.

As in my relationship with Sarah, the change was so gradual that I was completely oblivious to it until suddenly I was looking back and realizing that everything was different. Maybe the catalyst was when Becky started up classes at graduate school. Her work schedule changed to accommodate her coursework, and suddenly our blocks of available freetime didn't overlap as much as they had before — which was, incidentally, the same problem I'd had with Sarah, all over again; maybe I should have just quit my fuckin' late shift restaurant job, it caused me loads of problems and wasn't worth it. I just stayed there because it was a means to an end, a step on the ladder towards a better managerial position at a different company, once I'd racked up a few years of experience managing at the restaurant.

The amount of time that Becky had available to spend with me was further affected by the homework she now had, for her new classes. At first she slacked on the schoolwork, but that caused her to panic shortly afterwards. Then she started scheduling her time carefully, dividing her days up between school, her job, and me. But after she'd been doing that for not too long, it started to get to her; she got all stressed out.

I could tell that she was stressed, because she was kind of pissy; so when she tried to start an argument with me one night, I wasn't having any of it, I stayed calm and asked her what she was upset about. Eventually she said, "I need more time to myself." Well of course, I could totally understand that, I need a lot of solo time, too, and I told her so. Of course, I got plenty of alone time while Becky was at school, but after that conversation, I tried to be conscientious about what time of the day I called her on the phone, so I wouldn't interrupt her studies; and I didn't complain when I noticed that I didn't get to see nearly as much of her as I would have liked. I just asked her to call me when she had time to hang out. She promised that she would.

The thing was, as time went on, I started to suspect that she *wasn't* calling me when she had free time. After a couple of weeks had passed, I found that I was hardly seeing Becky at all, not even enough to satisfy my sexual needs, I had to resort to masturbation to get off, it was pretty frustrating. I would have liked to even just *talk* with her more often than I did, but I found that most of the time, if we talked on the phone, it was because I called her and caught her at a good time. She didn't call me too often. Sometimes she returned my calls, if I left a message for her when she didn't pick up; but more often, she didn't.

I should have taken the hint, I suppose; but a fool in love is the most foolish fool of all.

Well, it's obvious from this perspective, isn't it. She was shutting me out. I was going through a difficult time, and she didn't want to deal with my bullshit and my complicated feelings. I'd lost my novelty, and she was looking to move on. This was not immediately clear to me, however; for on the infrequent occasions when I *did* see her, she made no indications of it. Quite the contrary: Becky insisted sincerely that she was serious about our relationship, and that she cared for me, and blah blah blah.

But *then*, one night she's basically like, "Well, I had planned to study Biology this evening, because I have a quiz on Monday; but I'm going to put it off so I can go to this party." And I knew she was going with a gang of guys; but I also knew that if I said anything she would swear they were all "just friends," devoid of sexual potential: so I didn't say anything, because really I had no choice but to be okay with it; she wasn't asking for my opinion.

But that's all right, I figured, *even if she goes out with other people tonight while I'm at work, she can make it up to me tomorrow night, on Sunday.*

We had made formal plans two weeks previously to go out for a really nice dinner, and I'd really been looking forward to it. I cleaned my apartment and ironed my clothes days ahead of time. I bought extra candles and a new romantic CD, and I made reservations at a really posh place that we both liked but could rarely afford.

So, having been planning this date for two weeks, and having discussed it with her on the telephone just the previous evening, there I was on Sunday night, looking at my watch and thinking, *Well, she's ten minutes late, but I expect she'll show up any minute now,* when the phone rang. I answered it with some trepidation, fearing that it might be Becky calling me from her place. My fears were justified.

"Oh, I almost forgot," she said, "we were supposed to have dinner tonight, weren't we?"

"Yes," I said as coldly as I could, because although I was still battling denial, I knew what she was going to say next.

"I'm really sorry, Brandon, but I can't make it. I've got this Biology test tomorrow, and I really have to study for it."

"You mean, the test that you've had the last two weeks to prepare for?"

"For your information, mister, the professor added a bunch of new material halfway through last week."

"But you had plenty of time to go to that party with your *friends,* last night," I said jealously, like a weak wimp, like a wet and dirty discarded washcloth.

"*That* has nothing to do with *this,* Brandon," she lied, "now don't go getting all jealous on me. I've got a lot going on right now, and I don't need to be trying to deal with your issues all the time."

Well, I hadn't intended to write out all these conversations; but you can see where *this* one was going. I tried not to get upset, but of course I was; and I tried not to sound pleading, when I asked her to spend more time with me: but of course I sounded like a pathetic whiner.

And still Becky maintained the pretense. She told me that she truly wanted a real relationship with me, and that she would make time for me really soon. I was all wrapped around her finger, I so wanted to believe her. Becky swore her love to me, and solemnly promised to make it up to me; and, of course, like a deprived addict, I stubbornly clung to the hope of getting another Becky fix, someday, some sunny Sunday: although by then I should more reasonably have been trying to get used to the idea that I was going to have to go cold turkey and quit Becky for good.

As it turned out, the next afternoon after her test she did give me a blow job to make up for the missed date.

Nonetheless, as time went by, our relationship was still only *occasional*. Sometimes she would sleep with me; but sometimes she would promise to sleep with me, and then not call me for weeks. When we did talk, she *told* me over and over that she wanted to be with me; and like a complete idiot, I believed her. Becky liked to keep me in the "maybe" zone, where she knew she could keep me hanging on with very little encouragement. She was playing me like a poorly tuned instrument: she fingered my chords, and I twanged horribly. I'm really not sure what her point was in keeping up the pretense all that time.

One day, she met me for a brief lunch at the Wooden Spoon, then dodged out again with an excuse. We didn't get to spend any time alone, and certainly no sex, not even a quickie in the bathroom. It had been a long time. I was pretty frustrated, and frankly I was having difficulty in fighting off my suspicions that Becky was getting her satisfactions elsewhere.

Well eventually more than a week had passed since the last time I'd even talked to her, and she hadn't returned my calls in the meantime. I was belatedly beginning to realize that Becky did not want me anymore; but I was annoyed that she hadn't bothered to *tell me* so: and I wasn't about to oblige her by just conveniently disappearing from her life without leaving any residue. I had to validate my existence, for my own peace of mind. If I was going to get brushed off, I wanted to at least leave a big nasty grease stain that wouldn't come out in the wash.

And that's why I eventually called her at work one day, like an asshole. Yes, I looked up the zoo's number in the friggin telephone directory, and called there, and navigated the automated phone system until I got through to an operator, who put me on hold for a while, then transferred my call to another extension, where I was immediately disconnected. So I called back, went through the whole thing again, somebody answered the other extension this time, and when I asked for Becky they put me on hold for more than five goddamn minutes, except it wasn't really hold, they just put the handset down on the desk, and I could hear the message being passed around that Becky had a phone call, and then there was just the noises of people talking, and people walking by, and I sat there listening to the sound of the zoo ticket office bustle for a while, for a really long time in fact, until finally the phone got picked up with a clatter and Becky's voice said, "Hello?"

She didn't sound glad to hear from me. I'm sure I'd interrupted her in the middle of something, which is why it had taken her forever to get to the phone; but at least she agreed to meet me for dinner that night.

*   *   *

We met at a restaurant, not the Wooden Spoon but neutral territory, a sit-down Mexican diner that we'd never been to together. She was late. I had already finished a beer and ordered another by the time she arrived. I had begun to think she was going to stand me up when she walked in the door.

Still, even after all that, I tried to begin the conversation nicely. I asked how she'd been, how she was getting on with school and work and the people she saw there.

"Fine," she said tersely, and did not offer to expand on this.

137

Well, I figured, may as well just skip the bullshit and get down to it. "Becky," I said, "I'm unhappy with this situation. I live just across town from you but I hardly ever see you these days. I've really missed you a lot," I concluded, trying not to sound like I was accusing her.

"I've been really busy," she said.

"I know you have, and I'm sorry if it's stressful, but I guess I thought we were going to make an effort to spend time together."

"Hmmm," was all she said. She was looking at the menu. I let the silence continue, hoping Becky would break it, hoping she would realize how uncomfortable she was making everything. I was hoping she would exhibit some symptom of caring.

The waitress came and took our orders. After she left, Becky sat wordlessly in her chair, looking at her hands, for all the world like a child who's been sent to the principle's office to be scolded for something that was not her fault. The waitress came back with our drinks and appetizer. Becky still hadn't said anything. This was ludicrous.

"Becky," I said finally, "tell me what's going on."

She looked up as though she'd been waiting for this moment and said vindictively, "I think we should open our relationship back up."

"You do?" I said. "Why?"

"I've been feeling really trapped and constricted, and I don't like it. I feel like you're really demanding, and I just really need more space."

"You need more space?" I repeated incredulously. I was mad now. "What do you mean you need more space? I haven't seen you in weeks! How much space could you possibly need?"

"I've got a lot going on, Brandon, you can't be placing all these demands on my time–"

"But you haven't been spending any time with me at all!"

"But you have these *expectations*, and it's just more than I can deal with."

"And you're saying it would be better if we opened up our relationship?"

"Yes."

"You're stressed out because you don't have any time to spend with me, so you think it will help if I sit around with my thumb up my ass while you go out and spend a lot of time with a bunch of other guys."

"You can look at it like that if you want to," she said, her voice implying that I was being totally unreasonable.

"You haven't had sex with me in a really long time," I complained, "and now you're saying you want to have sex with somebody else." This wasn't opening our relationship up; she was replacing me, but trying to call it something else. But Becky persisted with the cover story:

"It shouldn't matter!" she protested. "Grow up, I don't need this irrational jealousy from you! It didn't used to matter, when we first hooked up, we had an open relationship with other people and by extension with each other, and it worked fine; but then *you* said it should be just us, and I went along with it at first: but now I'm starting to feel just way too constricted by the whole thing."

"Wait a minute," I argued back, "you can't say it was all me, you totally agreed, you were right there with me. I wish I could play you a recording of your voice. You said you wanted us to be each other's only ones, so it would feel special. You said that way, things would work between us. Remember that?"

"Well, I was wrong," she said with a shrug. "What else do you want from me?"

"I want you to be honest with me for a change," I said.

"I am always honest," she protested righteously.

"Look," I said, ignoring her lie, "I have to tell you that quite frankly I have been pretty dissatisfied with how much I've been seeing you lately. I don't see how this situation could possibly be improved by saying I don't care if you spend a lot of time with some other guy or a bunch of other guys or whatever it is that you've got planned. You wouldn't have any time left for me at all. What's the use in pretending?"

"Well, Brandon, I'm still young, and I don't feel like this is a good time in my life to make any kind of commitment to anybody, right now."

"Commitment? What did I say about commitment? Jesus, woman, I'm not asking you to marry me or something. I just had been thinking," I continued, trying to keep my voice calm, "that if you're actually my girlfriend, that I would like to see you occasionally, maybe even make love once in a while; and if it's not too much trouble for you, I really do think that it feels closer and more meaningful if we're only doing it with each other. That shouldn't be so hard."

"You don't make it sound hard, and I like you a lot Brandon, really I do, and it's wonderful when we make love together, but it's not as simple as that."

"Yes it is."

"No, it's not."

A protracted silence ensued. The waitress brought our food and stared at us curiously. We both said, "Thank you." We ate in silence.

Finally I said, "So you've met somebody else then."

"Don't jump to conclusions."

"Why beat around the bush? It's the only logical conclusion."

"You're being paranoid."

"Tell me I'm wrong."

"You're wrong."

But she wasn't looking at me, she was looking at the food on her plate, which she was turning over and over with her fork. I grabbed her hand and made her look me in the eye. "Tell me you haven't been having sex with anybody else," I said.

She looked down and didn't answer.

"I see." I chugged down the remainder of my beer, then caught the waitress's attention and ordered another.

"Look, don't get all huffy and self-righteous," she said.

"I didn't say anything at all."

"It's how you're acting. You send out these vibes."

"No," I retorted childishly, "it's not how *I'm* acting, it's how *you're* acting: you're acting callous, and unconcerned for my feelings, and dishonest, and downright just plain not very nice."

"Well, then maybe we should break up," she said, her face expressionless.

"Maybe we should," I agreed.

"If that's how you want it," she said, "then fine."

"It's *not* how I want it, Becky," I said, as if there were some point in explaining any more. "I love you, and I wanted us to be wonderful together. I guess it's not what you wanted."

"I *thought* it was what I wanted," she said softly.

"But now it's not."

"I don't know what I want. My life is so complicated!"

"I know what you want. You want some other guy, and you want him badly enough that you don't care whether or not hanging out with him will cause you to become completely, totally and permanently separated from me."

"We could still be friends," she said to me. God, I hate that line. It's such a cheap and shitty way of avoiding the situation. I felt as if she had just said, "Okay, I'll pretend that some mutual affection will always exist between us, if you'll promise to never, ever call me."

"Still be friends? What kind of shit is that?" I said, a little more loudly than I'd meant to. Just at that moment I realized the waitress was standing right next to me. She had brought my beer. She had a choked expression on her face, and was clearly trying to pretend that she hadn't heard my outburst. "Thanks," I said to her. She nodded mutely and moved away.

"Well, Brandon," said Becky coldly, as if this last point proved something she had suspected all along, "if you can't be my *friend*, then I don't know what the point is anyway."

"Just stop talking, will you?"

So we sat there in silence while I drank my beer and Becky drank her tea and chased her food around her plate. But finally I couldn't stand it any more, and I brought it back up. I wasn't ready to leave it alone. I wanted to take all the anguish I had caused Sarah, and add it to all the guilt I still felt, and distill the essence of all that pain, and pour it out on Becky.

"Why did you lead me on for so long?" I demanded.

"I wasn't leading you on," she said, "I really thought it was what I wanted."

"But you haven't called me, you haven't even returned my calls!"

"Because I didn't want to deal with this kind of stress."

"What's stressful about a guy you never see?"

"*This* is stressful," she said, "you are stressful right now, you're being really intense."

"I'd be a lot more relaxed," I accused resentfully, "if you hadn't just shown up & announced that you've been fucking someone else & that you're moving me out of your life to make room for him."

"If you want to see it like that, then that's your choice."

"No, Becky, this is your choice, you can't pawn it off on me, you're the one who's making this decision and you've been making it for quite some time."

"I don't want you to go away, Brandon," she said, although why she would have said that when I was acting this way is beyond me now.

Not only am I a total asshole, and completely selfish: I am also such a total sucker. "Convince me that that's true," I said, "because I don't want me to go away, either."

"I can't convince you of something you don't want to believe."

"Just tell me what it is that you want."

"I've been telling you that."

"There was no place for me in what you told me."

"If that's the way you want it..."

Well, shit, I don't remember what all we said. It was a stupid argument, and once it got past a certain point, it went predictably round & round, each of us repeating ourselves & attacking the other's logic, until finally we got up & left the restaurant and walked over to our respective vehicles in a strained silence.

I watched Becky unlock the car door. "Well, goodbye then," I said.

"Goodbye," she replied in a clipped tone. She looked at me for the briefest of moments, an unreadable expression frozen on her beautiful face.

Then she got into the car, started it without looking at me, and drove off.

*   *   *

That's just about the whole thing.

I guess after I lost all three of my lovers to other men, it didn't really surprise me all that much when I lost my job too.

What happened is, Nicky just stopped showing up for her shifts, she didn't come in one day, and then she didn't come for two weeks, and I had to mention it to the owner, because he kept putting her on the schedule, so he freakin called her on the telephone, and she told him that she quit, and then she told him about me, I think she sort of intimated sexual harassment, which isn't technically true, or okay I suppose technically some people might say that it *is* true; but regardless of that, more importantly she told my boss about the time when she and I had fucked on the floor of his office. I think that was what really pissed him off. I got fired, no severance pay or anything.

I don't know what I'm going to do. The economy's not doing so great right now, and I don't know if I can get much of a job, with no reference from the great job I'd had for the past several years; and I don't know how I'm going to get a place to stay without a job, after I move out of this place, which I have to start doing tomorrow.

But I'm trying to be optimistic about the whole thing. I'm trying to look at it as a chance to start over again.

Tomorrow is Day One of a new phase in my life.

Even so, for the rest of my life, I will never forget. I was involved with three amazing women; I loved and hurt them all; they all said they loved me, and they all hurt me, too, in their own ways; not that I didn't deserve it, I'm sure. I feel terrible, and pathetic because I love them still. I can't stop loving just because everything got all fucked up. The memory depresses the hell out of me. I just try and tell myself that I will handle it better next time, when I figure out what Next Time will be.

But right now it seems that even the best Next Time will be just a shadow of my former happiness. I fucked it all up, and nothing will ever be the same again. I had so much going for me, I didn't know what to do with it; and now that I've lost it all, I see no hope of regaining even a portion of my lost paradise.

I miss Sarah. Sarah and I broke up months ago, but still I think about her every day. Though we'd had other lovers before we met, she and I were each other's first real loves, and over the course of a relationship that lasted for four and a half years, we developed a deep trust and lasting friendship rooted in a shared innocence and the unbreakable bond of a love that we swore to each other would last forever. Once that trust was broken, the innocence became blighted and started to wither away. That lost innocence can never be replaced. Though I may in time find that I am capable of loving again, it will never, not for all eternity, be possible for me to love anyone the same way that Sarah and I once loved each other, because we were together during a formative time in our lives which will never come again. We never see each other any more, but we will always be a part of each other; and though I know she'll never come back to me, my heart still longs to sing her a love song.

I miss Nicole; and despite the anger that I still feel towards her, I also feel a lingering stain of guilt and disgrace that make me feel unworthy of being the recipient of anyone's love, ever again. I never meant to hurt Nicole; I just thought we could have a good time together. But hurt her I did, repeatedly, in a hundred thousand ways. I encouraged her to love me, and then I withheld reciprocity. I was careless and thoughtless and selfish; and, as she may never forgive me, I can only hope that some day she will be able to forget about me.

And I miss Becky. Oh, she hurt me so much when she left, I really felt like I didn't deserve to be treated like that (although perhaps some might say it was poetic justice for the way I had treated Sarah). I felt that I had been wronged, and I raged and I cried and I acted like a real dipshit; but my gods, I loved her so much, beautiful Becky and her perfect pussy. I miss her so much.

But when I turned on my stereo, there was a different song playing. I think it was by a band named Flumergex, or something; but they used to be called The Mushtones, apparently; and the lead singer was rumored to be certifiably insane. (Whatever. Most people are insane. The craziest fuckers out there are the ones who think they're *not* insane.) I liked his music though. The song was called "Another Go," and it went something like this:

Another Go

Baby I've lost everything for you
   and still you want another go.
It's such a bad idea,
   but your little ass is so sweet
     that I just can't say no!

Now I'm sweaty & sore from fucking you
   and still you want another go.
You've got fourteen other lovers,
   but your pussy is so sweet
     that I just can't say no!

Then the singer went into a bridge bit, and the drummer changed up the rhythm just a bit to match. It went,

> I lost my job and my wife
>> lost my whole friggin' life
> You stole my money and my dope
>> and you left me with no hope
> Now you've come back from the past
>> to offer me a piece of ass
> And I'm sure I've lost my mind
>> coz I still want you one more time!

And with that, the guitarist began evoking a series of agonized squeals from his distorted instrument.

*   *   *

But now it is late, and I have been abusing myself for days trying to get all this sick, twisted shit written out. I've done it, it's finished, and I must stumble off to bed.

When I awake, it will be the beginning of my new life. I will make everything good from now on. That is my vow to myself.

The night before Day One is over. Let the new day begin.

Sunrise